I0525928

INHOSPITABLE

ALI SEAY

Inhospitable © 2025 by Ali Seay. All rights reserved.

Grindhouse Press
PO BOX 540
Yellow Springs, Ohio 45387

Grindhouse Press logo and all related artwork copyright © 2025 by
Brandon Duncan. All rights reserved.

Cover design by Squidbar Designs © 2025. All rights reserved.

Grindhouse Press #110
ISBN-13: 978-1-957504-24-7

This is a work of fiction. All characters and events portrayed in this
book are fictitious and any resemblance to real people or events is
purely coincidental.

No part of this book may be reproduced, stored in a retrieval system,
or transmitted in any form or by any means, including mechanical,
electric, photocopying, recording, or otherwise, without the prior
written permission of the publisher or author.

GRIND
HOUSE
PRESS

G

WARNING

The following novella
contains infertility,
expectation of
pregnancy, early
pregnancy loss,
infidelity, violence,
body horror, and death.

In honor of all the women out there who exist under the weight of the ideas and expectations of others about what it is to be a woman.
I see you. Keep fighting.

And the vines they ever reach across the ground
And the branches in the trees they bend to make a crown
— The Builders and the Butchers

PROLOGUE

MAY 1981

THEY MOVED SO FAST SHE could hear them. The groaning and snake-like slither as they extended their reach and stretched for her. *Reached* for her.

Marielle fell and the fear slamming through her was like an electric current.

She let out a squawk that would have embarrassed her under other circumstances. Would have made her cringe if someone took her for a hysterical woman.

But right now . . . she didn't care. She was a hysterical woman.

The noises coming out of her were primal. All that mattered was getting away.

Something tickled her ankle, right above her boot and sock, and she screamed.

It was a goatlike sound, making her give a hysterical little laugh after.

The sky lit up with hot white lightning and the trees stirred with storm winds.

"Go, go, go——" she grunted.

She pushed off and the thing touching her ankle had now wound around it, causing her to flail. For a second she thought she'd finally met her doom and her fate was sealed.

But the force of her fear and desperation, despite her petite body, pulled her free.

"Ha!" Marielle shrieked, feeling a dizzyingly primal rush of joy.

She ran.

If she could get to the main house. If she could get inside.

Find the kerosine.

Get the matches.

If she could just manage to——

Something snaked out from her left, snagging her boot. Pulling her back. She felt the scrape of it around her leg and felt her hopes plummet and her doom rush toward her.

"No! Nonononono . . ."

Gripping fistfuls of wet grass she tried to haul herself forward, mimicking a soldier crawl.

A thick cool tendril joined the first and together they tightened around her ankle.

"No! Goddammit! I don't want to join him. I don't want to carry you!"

She clawed at the cool damp earth and, as the sky opened, a cold, violent rain came down on her. More tendrils joined the first two and she knew she was done.

The main house called out to her. A shape in the very near distance. Soft interior light glowing in the windows.

Inside was the warmed plate she'd held for Cecil in hopes he'd come home. This was the third night in a row she'd kept a meal for him, hoping he'd just gone off in a funk. She'd left a game show on the TV, up next would come that show with the writer lady who solved murders.

She should be up in that house waiting for her husband. But he'd never come home to her. It had been days. And now he never would, not ever again.

She longed for her home and her husband. For how things had been before.

She felt the whip and slap as another green tendril found her and pulled her back. Back to the barn. Back into the night. Back to where they waited.

CHAPTER 1

BRISTOL FOLLOWED JACE'S CAR UP the long driveway.

"How the fuck are we going to plow this when it snows?" she muttered.

It didn't really matter, though. They both worked from home for the most part. If it snowed, well, that was what Zoom was for, wasn't it?

The trees on either side, lush with new sharp green growth, crowded the gravel path, creating a canopy overhead.

"Oh, I bet he's in his glory," she said to Dippity.

Dippity, like any good dachshund, gave her suspicious side eye and had a sneezing attack.

"I agree, there is a lot of pollen."

This was what happened when you let your husband take charge of finding your new house while you traveled for work. The townhouse they had been renting had caught fire, thanks to a neighbor

4

with a penchant for alcohol and fireworks. The fireworks display he'd set off in honor of his son's kindergarten graduation had caught fire to not one, but three of the homes on that block. Theirs, the one on the end, had burned the brightest.

She was forever grateful she'd been away and Jace had been visiting his mother with Dippity in tow.

"Now we'll be living his great country house dream," she told the dog.

But it could be worse. They could be strapped for cash with no place to stay. Instead, she was doing great with the children's books, he was doing great with investing people's money, and things were okay in their little world. This might be good for her writing after all.

Palatial land. An honest to God fucking apple tree out back. An old barn that had seen better days but maybe, just maybe, held potential.

Despite all that good, reception for their phones and internet. What could be better?

A baby perhaps, but really?

Jace thought absolutely yes. She thought maybe. Just maybe. After what happened last time, she wasn't sure she had it in her.

She wasn't truly sold on it yet, but there was room for discussion.

~

Dippity loved the new place regardless of what anyone else felt. He bolted up the long drive and barked his ass off while his owners wandered.

Jace held his hands up as if placating her already. "I know, I know, it needs to be painted. I figured we could do that together."

She eyed the fading white paint on the old farmhouse. She didn't want to admit it, but the way it was sun-faded, surrounded by vibrant green, made it look like something out of a novel and not real life. She liked it.

He was watching her. He grinned.

Jace had read her mind, and she hated it. But she laughed.

"You like it don't you?"

"Shh," she said. "Let's pretend I don't."

He took her hand, squeezed, and together they walked inside.

CHAPTER 2

SHE STOOD IN THE BARE living room with its old tall windows. Sunlight streamed through the best it could considering no one had most likely washed them in decades.

"What's the deal with this thing? Just from the looks of it, why has it been sitting here? Why hasn't it been sold, flipped, zhuzhed up, remodeled and turned into an Airbnb?"

He sighed. "Long story."

Dippity scratched at the screen door and yipped to be let in.

"I've got nothing but time, husband of mine. Hit me."

Dippity looked around once and, in a mad dash, headed toward the kitchen.

"Brand new house and he already knows the kitchen," Jace laughed.

"He's a hound. He knows where food should come from even if there isn't any in there yet. Now tell me."

Jace went to a box marked BAR and popped it open. He took out a bottle of nice Cabernet before reaching into a box marked KITCHEN and extracting two Solo cups. He poured them each a nice glug of wine and handed her one.

"To the house's history," he said.

"Oh boy," she said, clinking her plastic cup to his.

"This house sat here for the last forty-three years because of fear."

"Serial killer?"

"No." He smiled.

"Domestic violence?"

"Nope."

"Aliens?"

"Bristol!" he cried and drained his wine.

"Well, Christ on a cracker, tell me."

"Inhospitable surroundings."

"What?"

"The forest didn't want them," he said.

"Them? Who them?"

"The original owners, Cecil and Marielle McGee."

He laughed as Dippity came in, stood with one paw raised, and stared at them. A silent reminder that four o'clock was swiftly approaching and that was his dinner time, thank you very much.

"Not yet," Bristol said to him with all the seriousness she could muster.

The dog blinked and put his nose to the hardwood floor and began to follow a scent only apparent to him.

"So, they thought the forest didn't want them and the fucking house stood here for that long?"

He shrugged. "So the story goes."

"Who sold it to us?"

"A distant relative. In fact, the only one they could dig up. A great-great niece twice removed or something," he said with a shrug.

He poured out more wine and set the empty bottle on the floor.

"They just left?"

"They say she just left," he corrected.

"Marielle?"

"Yep. The husband was gone."

"Died?"

She listened to the *tip tip tip* of Dippity's toenails on the floor. Wondered what it would sound like if it were instead the footfalls of little bare feet on the floor.

She had a momentary vision of a small child, curly-haired like its father, bolting through the downstairs on bare feet. Belly poking out proudly above a diaper. Maybe a bottle in hand. Those toddling unsteady steps of a small child or an amateur drunk.

She turned back in time to hear her husband say, "No, he went missing."

CHAPTER 3

"YOU BOUGHT US AN UNSOLVED mystery house!"

Jace scooped up a box marked for the kitchen and headed that way. Bristol followed.

"Not an unsolved mystery."

"Did they ever find him?"

He set the box on the counter, hung his head, and sighed. "No."

"Oh my god!"

"She said he ran off."

"But?"

"What do you mean but?" he asked, opening the box before opening a drawer.

Distracted, Bristol said, "Don't put anything in those drawers until we clean them out."

"Ugh."

"Indeed."

This time, he scooped up Dippity, who had camped out waiting for his dinner.

Bristol prompted again. He wasn't getting off that easy. "But?"

"His friends said there was no way he'd leave their new house. Or more specifically her."

"So why would she think that?" Bristol asked.

She opened the fridge, spied a box of off-brand baking soda and nothing more.

"The realtor said his friends insisted she didn't think that but she was lying."

"Jace! Why would a woman lie about her missing husband? Ooh!" she cried, startling both her husband and her dog. "Maybe *she* killed him!"

"That was a thought for a while. Especially for the authorities."

"And then she wouldn't sell the land, claiming it as inhospitable so no one would stumble over her husband's body." She gaped at him. "Oh, my god. You bought us a fucking murder house."

He shook his head. "No. Just a house with some . . . history that may or may not be nefarious."

"Muuuuuurder history," she said.

Dippity barked and they looked at each other.

"Dinner," they said in unison, which made Dippity very happy.

CHAPTER 4

JACE CONCENTRATED ON MARRING SOME of their pretty country house windows with AC units while Bristol scrubbed the fridge and all the cabinetry. By the time they met in the living room and flopped down on their worn but comfy sofa they were both sweaty.

"I am too tired to cook," she said. "You?"

He groaned. "No cooking. There was a sub shop a ways down the road. Want to come?"

She shook her head. "You go grab food. I'll go make the bed. We're going to need it."

He groaned as if in the throes of ecstasy. "Oh god. Bed. Soft. Cozy. Next to my laaaady . . ."

He grabbed for her, and she dodged him. "Go get food! I'll make the bed. After we eat we can take showers."

"Showers!" He did his pleasure groan again and Bristol found

11

herself laughing.

She loved him so much. Their life. How they were together. They'd fought to be this happy and now they were. Did she really want to upset that balance with a baby?

Shaking off the thought, she nudged him with her toe. "Food! Now."

Once the truck was barreling down their oddly long driveway, she stood. "Let's look around for a minute," she told Dippity.

He gladly followed.

The gazebo was in better condition than it appeared at first glance. Only part of the roof had succumbed to the elements. She was fairly certain she and Jace could replace it together. The dog bounded up the two steps, spun in a circle, barking, and descended.

"Come on, you dingus," she said.

Dippity followed her down the overgrown path, stopping every few seconds to sniff something.

Halfway to the barn she noticed something off. But she couldn't put her finger on it.

Standing in the middle of the path she put her hand out in a stop motion and said, "Sit, Dippity."

The dachshund took pity on her and actually obeyed for once. He sat, tongue hanging out, watching his mistress.

What was wrong? Why was she stopping?

After a moment, Bristol shrugged and continued down the path, whistling for her short companion to follow.

He barked once and came after her.

That's when it dawned on her—what she was hearing. Actually, what she was *not* hearing. The sounds of the forest had stopped as she walked the path toward the barn. No sounds of birds or squirrels. No rustling, caws, or sounds of flapping wings. Not even cicadas singing in the summer heat.

Nothing.

A very still, unsettling silence.

"I need to stop freaking myself out," she said. "They heard us coming so we spooked them. That's all."

CHAPTER 5

JACE FOUND HER IN THE barn staring up.

"Here you are!"

"Here I am," she said, only half listening.

Her eyes were still tracking the dense patchwork of vines lining the roof's interior.

"It's something, isn't it?" he said.

"It is. But how in the hell can we know if that roof is intact and safe if it's covered like that? And why are they growing inside? I thought they only grew outside."

Her husband shrugged and she covertly rolled her eyes.

Dippity repeatedly looked up at the vines, looked at her, and whined a little before spinning in his signature circles. She shushed him.

"I mean, you do hear about them getting in chinks in people's houses. Growing through the bricks and eventually into the house."

True. He wasn't wrong.

"It's just so weird," she said. "And lush, might I add."

Jace laughed. "It really is. I was surprised when Phil brought me out here too."

"Phil?"

"My college buddy. Our realtor."

"Ah. And did you manage to finagle any off this place because of its intense indoor canopy of vines?"

He shook his head. "Baby, this place was already at a rock-bottom price. The only thing that could have made it cheaper was if it had collapsed while we were looking at it."

"Speaking of collapsing," she said.

"Don't worry. I already called Vinnie and asked if we could borrow some of his scaffolding."

"Oh boy. Guess I should measure you for a body cast."

"Funny."

She grinned at him. But it really wasn't. Jace was a bit of a klutz. Hopefully, his brother Vinnie would help him out. Or maybe she'd take on this particular task, arguing with her less than graceful husband that she was lighter and therefore the better bet.

Her stomach grumbled, reminding her he'd returned with food.

"Follow me to your Italian cold cut sub and extra greasy sub shop fries," he said, taking her hand.

"My knight in shining armor."

Dippity, hearing the word fries, which he knew as well as "dinner," "walk," and "bath," took off running ahead of them.

"I think he wants a fry."

"I think if he gets there first we won't get any fries," she said, and they took off at a slight jog.

The food was perfect. Simple sub shop fare chased down with ice cold fountain Cokes and accompanied by complimentary chocolate cake.

"A welcome to the neighborhood from the owner, Titus."

"I like Titus," she said, groaning after the first bite of rich cold cake.

They followed all of this with quick showers and slow, easy, exhausted people, we-just-moved-into-a-new-house sex.

She woke at three a.m. not because of a noise but because of what seemed to be a sudden silence. It was deafening.

CHAPTER 6

SUNDAY

JACE DROVE BACK TO TOWN to get more of their stuff. Bristol decided to stay home. Her head was pounding, and she hadn't slept well. He'd offered to take Dippity but the dog was loath to leave Bristol. When she was under the weather, that dog was always by her side.

He'd promised her pastries from the bakery by their old house. The few things remaining in storage had survived the fire. They'd lost about half their possessions either to the fire, the smoke, or the water. Luckily some of their most important and treasured things had been on the lower floor and the fire hadn't quite reached them.

The phone rang and he took the call with a push of the button on the steering wheel.

"How's she liking it?" Phil asked. They'd known each other in college and had reconnected at a party after Phil started selling houses.

"Great so far! Knock wood, throw salt, and all that."

"What did she say about the barn roof, or has she gotten that far yet?"

Jace laughed. "Oh, come on. This is Bristol. She saw it. I'm pretty sure she thinks it's creepy."

"Well, it is kinda creepy."

"It is. But it's cool, too, right? We're overlooking the coolness factor?"

"No, it's also cool. You're both right."

"You wouldn't want to help me climb up there and see if the roof is intact and safe would you?"

"Fuck no!"

"Not even if I bought you pizza and beer?"

"Jace, my friend, there is not enough pizza and beer on Earth. Ask Vinnie, he's not afraid of heights."

"Don't worry. He's my next call."

Vinnie immediately said yes. Yes to scaffolding and yes to climbing up there.

"Man, I can't wait to see this. The way you're describing it sounds amazing."

"You're a weirdo," Jace said. But he laughed with relief he wouldn't have to climb up there and risk his life alone. "I'm going to shoot you some pictures when I'm not driving. You can see it in the photos but it's nothing compared to real life."

"It never is, brother," Vinnie said.

"Tell Ma we'll invite her up once the house doesn't look like a bomb went off."

"Will do."

They disconnected and Jace headed to his new home, a big pink box of pastries next to him in the passenger seat, a load of their remaining stuff in the back of the SUV.

This house was perfect for kids. Maybe the crazy neighbor with the fireworks had done them a favor.

CHAPTER 7

BRISTOL CARRIED A LOAD OF clothes down to the basement. She'd taken some ibuprofen and had a big glass of iced tea. Between the caffeine and the pain reliever she felt human again. They needed clothes though. She had most of them packed up in bags that had somehow conveniently ended up at the bottom of the pile. It would be easier just to wash some.

"Providing you work, you dinosaurs," she said.

The appliances looked brand new despite being from the eighties. Proof of that was their lovely shade of avocado green.

"This place *is* like a murder house," she said aloud. "No idea what happened. Everything frozen in time. Just kind of spooky."

She wished she'd brought Dippity downstairs. At least she wouldn't feel like a crazy person talking to herself.

She turned the machine on while it was still empty, allowing for the fact that after all this time the water might be muddy. Jace assured her Phil had tested all the appliances before showing the house, but she liked to err on the side of caution.

The water came out perfectly clear, so she dumped in some soap and once it had agitated a moment, she let her armful of clothes drop into the water.

It was the first time she'd been in the basement, and she found the space oddly welcoming. The walls were stone. Actual honest to god stone with mortar. A charming view when you're used to drywall and plasterboard.

She ran her hand along the cool stone. It would be the perfect place to put up canned goods. Learning to preserve food was on her bucket list. Something she remembered her grandmother doing when she was a kid. Bristol would always complain about how hot the kitchen was.

"Why do you have to in the summer when it's so gross?"

"Because that's when the vegetables and fruits are ready and ripe," her Grandma had said. "And those are the delicious things we want to eat when it's cold and gray outside in the winter."

Bristol would give anything for a jar of her grandmother's home-made apple pie filling and a spoon right now.

Instead, something small and gray ran across her foot and made her shriek.

Upstairs, Dippity gave a resounding answering bark.

"I'm okay!" she yelled to the dog but really more to assure herself. "Just a mouse."

She bent at the waist and surveyed the spot where the creature had come darting out. A gap about an inch or two at the base of one wall. A piece of wood that had served, presumably, as a baseboard had come loose with age, no doubt. She squatted down to look and nearly tipped over.

Finding herself on hands and knees she looked into the gap. Bristol gave a little shiver. Mice didn't bother her any—not really—but the sight of a mouse nest did for some reason. All that shredded paper and fabric.

"And poop," she said. "Don't forget poop." She wondered if mice really pooped in their nests. That seemed a bit counter intuitive, didn't it?

Then she spotted something else.

Bristol squinted. What was that thing?

It looked like a long metal box.

She sat back on her haunches and looked around. In the corner, only minimally dusty, was an old broom. She got up with a grunt, snagged it, and bent again to sweep the handle beneath the stone wall. Mouse scraps came out first.

"Sorry!" she yelled to the family she had just possibly displaced. "Very sorry." Then the drag and grind of a metal box over a poured concrete floor.

She stared at it for a moment. A gunmetal gray box with a handle and a latch. No lock, she noted. Whatever was in there she'd be able to get to.

"What are you?" she asked. "This really is a mystery house. Missing owners and boxes hidden in the walls."

Dippity started barking and she grabbed the box by its handle. The way he was barking, someone was here.

She passed the chugging washing machine and tugged the string to turn off the light as she started up the steps. She'd come clean up the mouse mess later.

And put down some traps. She didn't mind mice, but she didn't necessarily want to share her home and food with them. There was plenty of room out in the woods for them to live.

CHAPTER 8

THE VISITOR TURNED OUT TO be a short white woman with long greasy gray hair and a housedress that had seen better days and an equally threadbare flannel shirt over top. She stood with her face pressed to the screen. Bristol blinked and plastered on a fake smile.

"Hi, um . . . hi there. Can I help you?"

She started toward the door and Dippity gave a short growl. She hushed him and stood at the screen door making no move to unlock it just yet.

"You buy this place?"

Bristol cleared her throat. Swallowing the response of *what the fuck is it to you*, she smiled. "Yes. Just moved in yesterday. Or started to, anyway." She laughed.

"You should leave."

Bristol blinked again and felt her smile falter. "Ma'am?"

"Margaret," the woman corrected. "I live the next lot over. Not

20

very close but close enough to know someone made the stupid mistake of buying this place."

"Ma'am—"

"Margaret!"

"Right, Margaret. I'm not sure why this is any of your business."

"If you're smart, you'll go."

"Well, it's a bit too late for that now, isn't it?"

"You'll be sorry."

Bristol felt her hackles go up and straightened her posture. "Marga-ret," she said, emphasizing the syllables. "Is that a threat?"

The woman shook her head and gave a disgusted cough. "It's the truth."

Just then, Jace's car pulled up and he tooted the horn at her.

Bristol waved a hand and the woman took a step back. Bristol pushed through the screen door and walked out onto her porch.

"Margaret," she started.

"Be smart and leave," the woman said. "Don't say I didn't warn you."

She stomped off, her corduroy slippers covering her white socks that had lost all elasticity. She was a real looker, that Margaret, Bristol thought meanly and shook her head.

"Who was that?" Jace yelled, lifting the trunk lid.

"A welcoming neighbor," Bristol said on a laugh just a wee bit on the hysterical side.

He gave her a look and cocked an eyebrow. "You good?"

"Yeah, I guess I'm just suffering the effects of this week in general."

"Tired?"

"Very. How did the conversation with Phil go and are we getting scaffolds?"

"Fine and yes. He won't be helping me though. He's afraid of heights. Pussy."

"You're afraid of heights," Bristol said.

"Yeah, I know. I'm a pussy too."

She grinned and grabbed a box. "I'll do it if you want."

"Ooh, show off. Not afraid of heights. Going up on high things."

She shook her head. "What about Vinnie?"

"Vinnie'll be up there before giving it a second thought. Who was that woman?"

"Mar-ga-ret!" she said with exaggerated annunciation.

INHOSPITABLE ~ ALI SEAY

He shook his head. "I take it you didn't get along?"

"Not even a little bit. Maybe my good buddy Margaret is what they meant by inhospitable. Let's get this car empty. I'm starving."

"Me too. And we still don't have any food."

"We can hit the grocery store," she said. "It'll be fun. A little field trip away from getting this house in order."

"Sounds perfect. Maybe we can find a liquor store, too."

"You better believe it."

CHAPTER 9

BETWEEN THE VISIT FROM MARGARET and the trip to the grocery store she'd forgotten all about the box.

They'd ended up hitting the hardware store while in town and grabbing some charcoal. They had a small portable grill Jace had put out back on top of an old built-in brick grill.

"Eventually, I'll clean this up and get a new grate for it, but for now, it can hold our tiny grill in style."

She made corn and cucumber salad while he grilled chicken thighs and baby potatoes. They sat on the back steps side by side and ate while Dippity pranced back and forth at the foot of the steps demonstrating his desire to partake in the meal.

"So, what do you really think of it here?" Jace tossed Dippity a cooled piece of potato.

The dog dove for it, examined it, and refused it since clearly there was meat to be had. Then he must have remembered he was a dachshund and would eat anything and gulped it down. Bristol took pity on him and tossed him a piece of chicken. His tail going a million miles an hour, he dipped his long snout and the chicken disappeared.

"Kiss ass," Jace said.

She snorted, almost choking on her chicken. "He needs meat. Right, baby?" she said to the dog.

"You didn't answer me."

"I like it. So far. It's still sort of a shock. But I think we can make it nice here. I can even start canning. Have you seen the basement?"

For a flicker, she remembered the box before Jace said, "Yeah. It's awesome." His face shifted and she braced herself. She knew that look. "Speaking of babies."

"Were we?"

"Well, you were addressing your current baby," he said, dipping his head toward the dog repeatedly licking the stones to see if maybe additional chicken would materialize.

"Ah, him. See, I can leave him alone. I can do Zoom meetings without him screaming. He doesn't poop and pee directly on me." She eyed the small creature. "Well, not usually . . ."

"Bris—"

"I know. I know. You're serious and I'm joking around. But I don't know how I truly feel. I know what we talked about when we met. And talked about *again* when we got married. But it's been hard, harder than we expected, and we're older and it's getting harder."

"I know. But do you still *want it*? A baby? A family?"

She sat back, plate balanced on her knees. "Do you want the truth?"

"Of course."

She studied her husband carefully. People said they wanted the truth but did they really? Sometimes the truth is worse than a lie. Or not knowing.

"I think we're a family already. And I'm not sure if I still want a baby."

It landed like a stone in the middle of them. A heavy cold weight that would be hard to retract.

He tried so hard. So hard to keep his face neutral. But in the end, he failed. A faint flicker of anger but mostly a wave of disappointment crossed his handsome features.

"I see."

Oh boy. The very formal "I see."

"You asked for the truth," she reminded him.

"I know. Thank you for being honest. I'm gonna get a beer. Want one?"

"Sure," she said on a sigh.

It was going to be a long night. The space between them had grown astronomically since she'd told him her truth. She could feel it like a yawning void.

And it hurt.

CHAPTER 10

SHE COULD HEAR THE CRICKETS outside and it didn't help her sleep. A city girl, the constant *chirp chirp chirp* drove her bonkers. It would take some time to get used to it, no doubt.

Making it even harder to sleep was the fact Jace had basically frozen her out all night. Not his intention, she was sure. He wasn't that kind of person. Which made it even harder because she knew she must have really hurt him to make him clam up all night.

They'd watched a decent horror movie in awkward silence, sharing a bottle of Merlot. She wished for more. More would have meant she'd be asleep right now instead of lying next to him wondering how much she hurt him, how long he'd be mad. Correction: upset.

I'm not mad, I'm just disappointed . . .

She nearly laughed at her internal monologue but managed to swallow it. She turned on her side, sighed, and finally sat up.

Why should she feel bad for how she felt? Things happened.

Things changed. They'd always said they'd live in the city. Near the convenience, culture, and things to do. And now they were out in the woods playing *Little House on the Prairie* in an old farmhouse with a fucking barn for God's sake!

Careful, you're gonna get yourself worked up and then you'll never sleep. Just let it go until the morning and then you guys can talk again.

Pushing into the bathroom, she sat down and peed by the glow from the nightlight on the wall. "Like that'll happen. You'll stew, get pissed, and pass out from sheer rage and exhaustion," she said under her breath.

The *tip tip tip* of toenails told her Dippity had heard her get up, and thinking there might be food in it for him, followed her into the bathroom.

"Shh, we'll go downstairs in a minute, you stalker," she whispered to the dog.

In the bedroom, Jace snored so loud he grumbled in his sleep.

Speaking of sleep, how did men do it when there was conflict? Why wasn't he stewing too? Why weren't they outright fighting until it was settled? Why was he in there sleeping like a snoring baby while she remained awake?

When she got downstairs, Bristol remembered the box.

CHAPTER 11

SHE RUMMAGED IN HER PURSE until she found a fast-acting weed taffy, bit off half to help her sleep, and chewed it up while opening the dusty metal box.

Inside were various items most folks wouldn't leave behind. A mortgage receipt book for Cecil and Marielle McGee. Two birth certificates. His birthday 12/1/55, hers was 3/28/57.

"A young couple in love," Bristol said.

The edible was kicking in fast and she let it relax her. Take some of the sting away from Jace's disappointment and anger.

Under the birth certificates was a marriage certificate.

"A lovely June wedding."

And then a birth certificate followed by a death certificate for a baby named Millicent Denise McGee.

"So sad," she said, meaning it. Then a bit bitterly, "At least you did right by him. Spat out a kid."

She snorted and felt shitty for laughing.

Head in hands, she groaned. What the actual fuck? Did they get a new house only to learn to hate each other because of a baby that never was and may never be?

She felt the sting of impending tears and repeatedly blinked her eyes to ward them off. She absolutely would not fucking cry.

Then she hit pay dirt. The ultimate distraction. A small leather-bound journal, smooth from wear. Inside, cream-colored lined pages with slanted, feminine handwriting.

Bristol grabbed her purse and rummaged until she found her readers. "What's in here, Mrs. McGee? Some juicy gossip maybe."

She turned to the first page.

Diary of Marielle McGee. May 1981.

She began to read.

CHAPTER 12

HE'S BEEN WEIRD LATELY. HE goes out to that barn all the time. Alone. The first time was to make sure the structure was sound. It's a bit older than the house, Cecil said. But then he kept going.

Almost daily he treks out there. I think it's to get away from me. At least I'm starting to think that.

Losing the baby was hard on us both but him shutting me out is even harder.

I cried myself to sleep last night because he didn't come home for supper and didn't come back at all until almost bedtime.

I wonder sometimes if he's meeting someone out there, but I don't think there's anyone around here for a ways but for Margaret and she doesn't have any interest in Cecil. The idea is laughable.

The only thing I can figure is he's mourning and doesn't want to share it with me and that's a hard pill to swallow.

I miss the baby too. The promise of her, I mean. She wasn't here but for a blink. Long enough to rip my heart out when she went. And his too it seems. But damn. He could be here for his wife, right?

Or am I being selfish?

My mother says I'm being paranoid. That men grieve differently than we do, and I can't expect him to be all emotional and caring. I say bullshit. You stick together in times like this. That's what marriage is.

I know we're out in the sticks, but sometimes after I talk to my mother, I'm glad we're far away out here and at the very least she's not around. Terrible thing to say but I'm sitting here laughing as I write it, so I guess it has some value after all.

The sun went down a while ago. It's going down later and later as summer creeps in. I think I hear him coming. I'll take a big breath and sit down while he eats the dinner I kept warm for him and see if he'll talk to me.

Or just hold my hand and kiss me for God's sake. If he can't share his pain with me he could at least bear witness to mine. Maybe try to lighten it some.

Life feels very strange right now. I hope it gets better soon.

CHAPTER 13

A **YAWN SPLIT HER FACE,** and she rubbed her eyes. She wanted to go on reading but heard the creak of the steps and Jace's soft voice talking to Dippity. She sat up straight, waiting.

He came in, looking sleepy and confused.

"Why are you down here?"

She had shoved the journal into her lap beneath the table. She wasn't sure why. A selfish gesture. Not wanting to share her find even with her husband.

"Couldn't sleep," she said. At least it was the truth.

"What are you doing just sitting there?"

She smiled. "Waiting for my edible to kick in fully so I can sleep."

He chuckled. "Ah-ha. Okay. Well, has it kicked in?"

He looked like he wanted to say more but kept silent.

She had a lot she wanted to say too.

I'm sorry . . .

How dare you . . .
My feelings matter . . .
I would be the body that carried it . . .
I might have changed my mind . . .
But not about you, never about you, please don't let this ruin us . . .
But just like her husband, she kept silent.

"Some."

"Then let's go to bed." He held out his hand.

An olive branch.

She stood, dropping the journal into the open mouth of her canvas tote slung over the back of the chair.

If Jace noticed, he didn't say anything.

"Okay, but only if you rub circles on my back for a few minutes."

Another chuckle. "Deal."

They walked up the steps together and Jace clicked his tongue. "Come on, Dippity Doo, you too."

The last thing she really remembered was the sound of Dippity's jaunty little taps up the hardwood steps.

Then she lay down and was out like a light.

CHAPTER 14

MONDAY

SHE DREAMED OF MARIELLE AND Cecil. Their dead baby. The barn. And something in the woods causing the animals and birds to stop making sounds. She woke up in a cold sweat to bright sunlight and the sound of noisy morning birds.

Jace wasn't beside her so she starfished, letting her arms and legs splay wide in a stretch.

The bedding shuffled, bounced, and suddenly a black and tan snoot came out from under the covers.

"Oh, I'm sorry, your highness. Did I disturb you?"

Dippity confirmed that yes, she had, but all was forgiven, when he began to lick her entire face including her eyelids.

"Okay, okay! Enough of that." She gently pushed him away. "Where is your father?"

That phrase, one she muttered almost every day, suddenly hurt her heart.

Your father.

Dippity leapt off the bed and she sat up. Her ears picked up the gentle hiss of running water. Mystery solved—Jace was in the shower.

She pulled on her leggings, knotted her too long hair on top of her head. She had to go for a cut, it drove her bonkers.

Then she took the steps slowly, feeling somewhat groggy and stiff. Once she put coffee on, things were looking up. The scent of dark roast filled the kitchen. Blinding sunlight showed how much cleaning they still had left to do.

Maybe today she would tackle the floors, and he could tackle the windows. They looked as if they'd been soaped to obstruct the view at some point. Probably smart for a house standing abandoned in the woods for decades.

She fed the dog, who was doing his starvation dance, and put two pieces of bread in the toaster. She wanted an egg sandwich, but they didn't have eggs. Or milk. Somehow, she'd forgotten these staples the day before. Another trip to the grocery store was in order. At least it would help her memorize the route and familiarize her with the area.

The stairs creaked with the sound of Jace's footsteps and Dippity looked up.

Her husband walked in fully dressed, surprising her.

"You're awfully spiffed up for a day of cleaning this woefully dirty house."

His face said there was another plan.

She waited for an explanation while doctoring her coffee with collagen powder, sugar, and a few of those creamer cups she'd stolen from the coffee shop last time she'd been. She kept them in a large jar for emergencies.

"Mom called and she needs a ride to her treatment. Her car's in the shop and Vinnie had a work emergency. So, it's me."

"Oh, okay. Well, do you think you'll be long?"

He shrugged and poured a mug of coffee, swigging the hot liquid as it was.

Bristol shivered; she couldn't help herself. Black coffee. Gross.

"Vinnie said sometimes she gets pretty sick, so I figured I'd stay with her and take her home after."

"Okay," she said. "How long is her treatment, usually? Do you need me to come with you?"

He smiled. "A few hours. I'm sure we'll be fine. I'm going to take my laptop with me. Maybe get some work done."

"Okay, keep me posted." When he kissed her, she kissed him back. It still felt weird between them. Stiff and awkward. She hated it.

"What are you going to do?"

She spread her arms wide. "Take your pick! Windows, floors, whatever gets my attention first."

"Don't go at it too hard. I'll be home to help you later."

His phone dinged with a text and he glanced at it. "Gotta go. I'll be home later. Love you."

One more peck on the cheek and he was gone.

Bristol looked down at the dog. "Well, shit."

~

The cleaning didn't last long. Bristol decided to take a shower and head to town for her forgotten grocery items. It would do her good, maybe help her shake off some of the weirdness from yesterday.

She put the dog in the kitchen and put the gate up in the doorway. His eyes said this betrayal was abysmal.

"Just until you get used to the house and I know you're not going to pee on everything or chew up my sofa. You act out, you little shit."

He sniffed at her, turned his back, and lay down in a sunbeam.

She grabbed her reusable bags and headed out to the car. They only needed those few things. And maybe something good for dinner—a steak perhaps.

As she left their driveway and turned onto the main road, a big red truck that had long ago faded out to nearly pink approached. It slowed as it passed. Going slow enough that not only did she get a good long look at the vehicle, but at the occupant.

Margaret.

The woman gave her a death glare before punching the gas. The truck rocketed off with the deep chuckle of an ancient engine still doing its job.

"Neighborly." Bristol turned up the radio. It took a minute for the goosebumps to leave her arms and thighs.

CHAPTER 15

THERE WERE A LOT MORE eyes on her today. Maybe they'd come during church service yesterday. Either way, here she was on a Monday afternoon being gawked at by what felt like half the town.

She did her best to give some small friendly smiles here and there and was met with a few in return, but a lot of people just stared.

It enticed her to make quick work of it.

Milk, half and half, a steak, some eggs, some corn that looked fairly good, and a bag of rice. She'd have to make a point to at least unpack their pantry items so she could truly take stock of what they had and what they needed. As an afterthought, she added some lunch meat, cheese, and yogurt so they had quick stuff to eat.

Near the front was a modest beer and wine selection. She added a 1.5-liter bottle of her favorite Cabernet and a six-pack of the microbrew Jace liked best. Her own peace offering.

She found herself staring at the gardening magazines in the

checkout line. They had so much land now, maybe they should try a garden. Better yet, a vegetable garden. Lofty goals for a woman who killed everything she touched.

Her eyes strayed to a tabloid talking about a hot young starlet starting her family "late in life." The woman was thirty-two. She, herself, was thirty-eight. That giant 4-0 just around the corner.

Jace, at thirty-six, was ready. She wasn't sure it would work. They had tried and failed, and the repeated failure had either cured her of her want or given her time to realize her lack of want.

Either way, it was a difficult thing examining her own feelings while trying not to be blinded by his.

"Miss?"

She looked up, realizing the person in front of her had paid and moved on.

"Oh, God. I'm sorry," she laughed and could feel heat coloring her cheeks. "I was daydreaming, I guess."

The kid looked to be about twenty or so and gave her a small smile. Finally, someone who could at least pretend to be hospitable.

"Did you find everything you were looking for?" he asked.

"I did. And then some." She eyed the pack of Haribo gummy bears that weren't on her mental list.

"You bought the McGee place, didn't you?"

"Yep, that's us."

"How is it?" he asked, seemingly genuinely curious.

"Old and dirty. I still have a lot of cleaning to do. Damn it!"

That's what she'd forgotten. Paper towels.

"Need to run back?" he asked.

"I do. Sorry. Maybe this will make it faster. What aisle are paper towels in?"

"Seven."

"Be right back!"

By the time she got back, he was ready for her. He scanned her last item, and she paid.

"Thank you," she said. "Sorry again."

"No worries. Have a good day."

His gaze lingered for a moment. Part of her—the oh shit, I'm thirty-eight part—wanted to believe it was because he thought she was pretty.

The intuitive part of her told her that wasn't it.

He looked concerned. That's what it was.

CHAPTER 16

SHE NEARLY DROPPED THE EGGS when her phone rang. It was at top volume for some reason, and it startled her.

Vinnie's face lit up the screen and she accepted the call, suddenly worried something had happened to Jace and his mother.

"What's up, Vin?"

"Scaffolding!" he yelled.

"What about it?"

"Jace wanted some and I'm calling him about it."

"He's with your mom at chemo," she said.

There was a pause and then Vinnie laughed. "Shit. Sorry. Don't have my head screwed on straight. Let's see if he answers. That's why I call you, doll face. You're reliable."

Then her brother-in-law disconnected.

She wasn't a fan of that pause. Or his confusion. Or being called doll face.

Her stomach sickeningly rolled over, and she took a deep breath before getting herself a glass of water.

"It's fine. He made a mistake. Jace would never do that. Not again."

She stared out the back door to the path leading to the back of the property.

Maybe she'd go for a walk. Look at the grounds. See if she might be able to grow something on her own. For herself.

She didn't call for him, but Dippity heard her open the door and raced after his mistress.

"You can come but you need to behave," she informed him.

His answer was to race down the trail ahead of her, barking his fool head off.

"Perfect."

~

When she got to the barn she realized she'd lied to herself. She wanted to look at it again after reading the journal. Why she hadn't read more of the journal was a better thing to ponder.

But she was here now, standing in the large open space littered with a few remnants of the life lived before her. Some old gardening tools leaned against the wall. What looked like hip waders slouched in the corner like a body relieved of its meat. And above her the whole time lurked the ivy, breathing its cool humidity into the space.

It was much cooler in the barn. Enough that she found it refreshing. Sitting down cross-legged in the middle of the space, she looked around. What could she do here? Could be as simple as creating an outdoor kitchen for canning. A summer kitchen her great-grandmother had called it.

He's cheating on you again . . .

Could be as intricate as some kind of office space so she could come out and work without interruption.

If you won't give him a baby, she will . . .

"Stop!" she hissed aloud. "Just let it be. Let it go."

He said he never would again but once they do it a first time it makes that second time soooooo much easier . . .

She concentrated on her breathing the way the therapist had taught her years ago. Inhale slowly through the nose. Hold for a count of four. Blow out forcefully through relaxed lips.

Despite all of this she felt the panic attack creeping in.

She suffered from them terribly after she'd found out about Jace and that woman from work. It was part of why he'd made the move to almost all telework. The affair, that was, not the panic attacks.

It was easier for Bristol to stay with him if she could set eyes on him most of the time. Especially in the beginning.

She stood on wobbly legs, fairy lights dancing in her peripheral vision.

"Breathe. Breathe. He learned his lesson. You're being paranoid. He wouldn't do that again. Breathe."

She walked out into the sun on legs that felt absent. That was too bright, so she walked to the side of the barn where the tree line started. Dippity bounded up to her and gave her the stink eye.

"Fine. It's fine. I'm fine."

She sat down, again following the advice of her former therapist who leaned toward the hippie, crunchy side. *When in doubt seek out nature.*

Putting her back against a tree, she shut her eyes and focused on her breath.

CHAPTER 17

THE DOG WAS LICKING HER.

Bristol tried to reach for him to push him away, but her arm met with resistance.

When she opened her eyes, the sun was lower in the sky than it had been and the dog was standing on her lap licking her arm.

An arm that was bound, albeit lightly, with a vine.

It had curled around her forearm and down to her wrist, giving her just enough resistance to wake her.

With a little cry of disgust, she grabbed it and yanked it off. She gave a full body shake and laughed wildly.

"It's just a plant, for fuck's sake."

Dippity barked and ran in a circle.

"Jesus Christ. Fuck!"

She stood, wiping herself off briskly to make sure nothing else had attached to her as she slept.

Dippity jumped at her, but he was tangled in the vines. She snatched him up and pulled his stumpy little legs free.

"You okay, buddy? Yeah? Who's my baby?"

He licked her face frantically, the way he did when stressed.

"Let's go home. I don't know how the fuck I dozed off mid panic attack. I guess I exhausted myself."

As she talked, she kicked her foot free of an encroaching vine and headed toward the trail.

She'd deal with the barn and the vines later. They really were getting out of control.

She practically ran down the path, realizing how much later in the day it was. How long had she slept there? It had to be fairly long for vines to find her. She knew how they worked, for the most part, waving in the wind until they found something to latch onto.

"Careful, girl, you're going to look like that barn roof." She laughed hysterically and shook her head. The fear Jace was up to his old tricks was getting to her.

It made her a little bit nuts.

CHAPTER 18

HE'D CHEATED WHEN HIS FATHER was sick. A woman he worked with named Karen.

She'd known Karen had a thing for Jace. Every work party showed her making eyes at Bristol's husband. Every time Bristol stopped by the office, the woman was there checking her out.

She never thought he'd fall for it. Jace, who claimed to love her more than life itself. Jace, who said his life didn't truly begin until he met Bristol.

Jace. Her Jace.

Cheater.

She'd found out by accident—of course. There was no confession here. She'd simply been doing laundry—it was her turn that month to do it—and noticed his jeans smelled like perfume. She'd been willing to give him the benefit of the doubt until she ran her hand through his pockets to look for any loose change or detritus and came up with a shiny foil packet for a condom. An *empty* packet.

They didn't use condoms. After all, the goal, especially for him, was to knock Bristol up.

And so, what the hell was that in his pocket?

He hadn't tried to lie. She'd give him that much. He had confessed the moment he'd been presented with the evidence.

His excuse was extreme stress, his father dying, blowing off steam, and he felt Bristol was removed from him emotionally. That she didn't want to build a family like he did. That she didn't want to build the life they'd talked about.

So, in a nutshell: Her fault.

There had been therapy and fights and tears and even a trial separation, but in the end, they had worked it out. With strict rules. Honesty above all else, communication, he'd work from home often, when going out he would explain where he'd be and always be reachable.

And they had gone on that way for years, until now.

Now, she stood in the kitchen watching her phone screen ring his number and there was no answer.

She thought about calling Betty, his mother, and checking what was going on, but emotionally, she didn't think she could. Not at the moment.

Bottom line: If he was cheating on her again, her brain and heart weren't ready to know just yet.

She fed the dog, scrubbed her hands vigorously, and when that didn't do the trick to remove the phantom feel of those intrusive little feet vines used to climb, she went to jump in the shower. She'd scrub herself head to toe and fix dinner. When he got home, she'd calmly try to suss out what was going on.

Calm being the operative word.

The water was hot. She soaped herself up slowly, taking long deep breaths of humid air and trying to shut down her racing mind.

If he was cheating, what would she do?

Kick him out?

Leave?

Pretty soon the time she'd set aside from her book deadlines for moving would be over and she'd have to function. Pretty soon she'd have to address this. Pretty soon she'd have to deal with her GOD DAMN CHEATING HUSBAND . . . AGAIN!

"Deep breaths, no rage," she reminded herself, but inside her wet

body anxiety and sadness warred with anger and loathing.
How could he?
Again.

CHAPTER 19

JACE TURNED HIS CAR INTO the driveway. Knowing he had plenty of driveway before he hit the house, he pulled to the side and put his head in his hands.

"What the fuck is wrong with you?" he sighed.

He'd sworn to himself and his wife years ago he'd never do this again. And yet here the fuck he was.

All due to his fragile masculinity. His wanting a child and his wife, maybe, possibly having changed her mind. So, he runs right out and gets his dick wet?

"Asshole," he seethed. "You're risking everything."

But what did he really have if he didn't have that dream? That dream they'd shared for so long.

Morgan had been flirting with him for ages. She bartended at The Piano Key downtown. The place he met coworkers and potential clients. A regular place no one would think about as odd.

She'd given him her number ages ago. Bending over the bar so he was sure to see the mile of cleavage she offered. Her dark hair falling around her shoulders. She was curvy and luscious and had eyes as blue as the sky in September. And she was hot for him.

Somehow, he'd managed to resist until the conversation he'd had with Bristol about the baby. Or lack thereof.

And he'd found himself shooting the lovely Morgan a text while his wife was in the bathroom. Careful his phone was set to "do not disturb" so as not to make any noise, he checked it frequently.

It only took about twenty minutes for her to answer and invite him to her place the following day.

He'd jumped at the chance.

Jace scrubbed his face with his hands. He'd been careful to shower well and not use anything but plain bar soap, but he was sure—absolutely positive—the stench of betrayal still clung to him.

Pussy and cum and infidelity.

He'd stopped by his mother's to have a cover story. Told her things were tenuous at best. Told her about the baby. Tried to get her on his side . . . just in case. In case Bristol found out and started to sniff around.

His mother hadn't been as sympathetic as he'd hoped and she'd been distracted by feeling so shitty after treatment.

That reminded him, he'd also have to talk to Vinnie in case he spoke to Bristol.

Such an easy slip up—so much coverup.

Starting the car, he realized it was well past their normal dinnertime. Hopefully, sympathy would earn him a pass. Being with his mother during her treatment had to be a good excuse for missing the normal dinner hour.

If only that's where he'd actually been.

CHAPTER 20

IN A SUNDRESS AND STANDING barefoot on a kitchen floor she'd scrubbed the bejesus out of, she was in a calmer place.

Maybe not so much calm as disassociated. Her therapist, the wonderful Sally Sidle, had told her she did it when life was too much and too real. She had encouraged Bristol to feel her feelings as much as possible.

She flipped the steak carefully, not letting the mix of butter and olive oil splatter her dress. She'd given Dippity a pig ear and he was lying on his bed chewing the fuck out of it.

At least someone was happy.

The microwave beeped, alerting her the green beans were done steaming. The only shortcut to the meal would be doctored instant mashed potatoes. She wasn't a diva, though, she loved those things. Grew up on them. She doctored them so well she'd won Jace over years ago to the wonders of the shortcut potato.

One more flip of the steak and she counted to sixty. She heard the grumble and pop of his tires on the gravel drive and felt no reaction. Definitely disassociating.

If she let herself feel her feelings right now, she might plunge the barbeque fork on the counter right into his fucking face.

But she wouldn't do that.

She wouldn't even accuse him because she wasn't sure. And she didn't really want to know at the moment. One hurdle at a time. The house was first, her figuring out what she wanted to do if her suspicions were true second. Her peace of mind and control of her own emotions must be stronger than her hurt and anger.

The front door squealed when he opened it.

They needed to remember to oil the hinges.

He walked into the kitchen with that look on his face. No doubt he was clueless that he looked guilty and worried. She saw it all in fast forward.

Her grabbing the cast iron pan, steak and all, and smacking him in the face with it. She could hear the searing sound of hot metal meeting flesh. Then burying the barbeque fork in his neck below his smoking, blistered face. Pulling it out of the meat of him, plunging it back in. Releasing all that traitorous blood in his body with a frenzy of plunging blows.

She smiled. "Hi there."

The worry fled his features and relief settled in its place.

"How are you, babe?"

"Starving," she said, meaning it. "You?"

"Same."

He smelled like soap. Not their soap. A man who'd been at the hospital all day with his cancerous mother shouldn't smell freshly of soap. He should smell like death and worry and grief. Maybe a hint of disinfectant and urine like any hospital. But not like soap.

Not *their soap* her brain piped in again. Not the stuff they use. Something else. Something more flowery.

"Great. Go wash up and we'll be ready to eat. Can you open the wine when you get back?"

"Sure."

He practically fled the room, which shouted about his guilt again. She pulled the steak off to rest, mixed butter and a bit of sour cream into the mashed potatoes, and pulled the green beans out of the microwave. A pat of butter, some salt and pepper, and they were all ready to go.

They could feast. She could eat and watch him try to appear normal. Watch him battle his guilt. Watch his stupid traitorous fucking face as he ate the dinner she'd prepared.

CHAPTER 21

SHE'D FUCKED WITH HIM A little. She had to have some fun or she'd absolutely lose her fucking mind.

"So, how's your mom? Did she do well at treatment today?"

She forked a bit of steak into her mouth, smiling sweetly like the good wife. He thought he was cool, but his face was a mask of worry and concern.

"She did fine. You know, cancer is hard."

He flinched when he said it. She nearly laughed.

Cancer is hard? Oh, is it, darling?

Bristol laughed into her hand and carried on eating. Her skin still tingled in spots from the greenery trying to grow around her. She must have really been dead to the world for it to think she was an inanimate object and thusly fair game.

"Should I call her? See how she is? Maybe I can take her one day. Lend a hand to Vinnie so he doesn't have to do the lion's share."

"Vin doesn't mind!" Jace blurted. "He likes to be in charge of her care. Those two are thick as thieves. Always have been."

"Good," she said. "I'm glad to hear she's doing okay. Still, I might call her this week just to say hi."

Just to make him squirm. But also, she hasn't reached out to Betty in a while and that made her feel bad. When the stuff about the affair had come out years ago, she'd been horrified her son had cheated on Bristol. She had been the epitome of motherly. Important given Bristol's mother died when she was in her early twenties.

"What did you get up to today?" he asked, blatantly steering the conversation away from his mother.

"Took another walk out to the barn. Hit the grocery store first. What a bunch of weirdos."

She swallowed hard, realizing how much she wished this was a normal conversation. Her chatting with her best friend and husband about the weird people in town instead of a cat and mouse game of "Can I Catch Him Lying."

Tears stung her eyes, and she blinked furiously to clear them. She stood, nearly knocking her chair over, and turned her back to him to wipe at the wetness on her face.

"More mashed potatoes?" she asked to cover her sudden movements.

She wanted to turn around and smack the hot silver pot upside his head. Maybe beat him until he bled, confessed, cried, and begged for forgiveness.

Instead, she dropped a green bean on the floor for Dippity.

"I'm good," he said softly.

He sounded sad.

Good.

When the farce of dinner was over, she told him she was taking a walk.

"Want company?"

"No, I'm going to see if I can find some wildflowers. Just be alone for a bit. Moving is hard."

She took her canvas tote off the chair presumably to gather some wildflowers. Inside, the weight of the journal was prominent.

She'd meant to read it after her walk down to the barn but had fallen asleep before everything went awry. Now, she felt a deep-seated *need* to read the thing.

And get away from her husband. Her anger toward him was

growing and starting to scare her.

He didn't talk to me. He never does. When we first married that's all we did was talk. We talked about life, people, religion, politics, the world. We talked about our future. What we wanted, what we didn't. We talked about getting a house, having a family, building something.

Cecil wanted to grow food. Our own. Be stable without the world which he said was a swiftly turning tide to greed and super consumerism. I laughed at him, but the older I got the more I saw his thinking. To be able to be a family. To be a unit. Out here and alone if need be. It had an appeal.

But now we're out here and my best friend doesn't talk to me. He acts scared a lot, but also enchanted for lack of a better word. Like whatever is scaring him is also wooing him? I know I'm not making sense, but I'm trying to pin words to a feeling I've never had and that's hard.

I thought we'd take some time to grieve the baby. To reconnect as a couple. We wanted to do big gardens but missed the window but right now we could do jack-o-lanterns and kale as small crops. Just to do something. I told him we could sell the jack-o-lantern squash by the side of the road during the fall. A buck each. It could be fun.

He nodded as if he were listening, shoveled down his food, drank about a bucket of water and seemed to constantly have his head cocked like a dog listening for something.

"Cecil, do you hear me!" I damn near shouted. He had because his head swiveled toward me oddly, his dark eyes as big as lanterns, and said, "I hear you."

"Do you still love me, Cecil?" I demanded.

And he broke my heart then because he said, "I think so."

I'm going to bed. Writing isn't helping me tonight.

CHAPTER 22

WEDNESDAY

THE SCAFFOLDING ARRIVED ALONG WITH one of her favorite people—her brother-in-law, Vinnie. His big work truck grumbled and spat its way up the driveway. But what was in the back were things that certainly didn't look like scaffolding.

"What's this?" she yelled, shielding her eyes from the sun when he climbed out.

"These are seven-in-one multi-purpose folding adjustable telescoping aluminum extension ladders."

"That's a mouthful."

"Absolutely."

He ran a hand through his hair and stretched his back dramatically.

Bristol gave him a hug, patting his back and he hers. They'd always gotten along brilliantly and she was so grateful for that. She never had siblings of her own so her relationship with Vinnie filled that need.

"Now tell me why no scaffolding."

"Those things weigh about a thousand pounds! No shit."

"No shit?" she echoed, laughing. "This thing will be good instead?"

"Should be. Let's get a look at this ceiling roof deal. Then I can tell you if we're fucked or not."

Together they walked into the coolness of the barn and her brother-in-law tilted his head back and let out a whistle. "What's that? Sixteen, seventeen feet?"

"I don't know," she said. "I haven't measured it. Why?"

"Well, the ladders I bought are eighteen feet. So, we need to be sure they'll reach. I'm guessing we'll be fine but only time will tell. I'm gonna back the truck up in here. Less lugging."

She nodded, studying the full, lush green canopy overhead. It still bothered her there was no sunlight for the vines in the barn. Not really. Some negligible light from the old dirty windows and obviously some when the barn doors were open, but not a lot. Not *enough*, surely.

The rumble of the truck filled the small space, and the taillights glowed red demon eyes in the gloom as Vinnie backed up.

He cut the engine and climbed out, wiping his forehead with a handkerchief from his back jean pocket.

"Only June and already gonna be a ball-melter of a summer."

She snorted. "I wouldn't know."

"Well, whatever ball equivalent you have," he said, laughing.

"Let's get these out and set up. It's a two-man job for sure."

He put the tailgate down and attached a ramp. With a lot of swearing and grunting they managed to get the two ladders out and began to unfold them.

"Jesus, Vin. You need a degree to know how to operate these things." She pushed part of the segmented ladder flat.

"You get the hang of it when you use them all the time. Put the safety pin in."

She pushed the thick metal pin with a flat plastic cap through the hole he indicated.

"Makes extra sure it doesn't dump your ass on the ground."

"Wonderful!" she cried, making a face at him.

"Look, lady, every time you do something like this, go up high and all, there's a risk. It's just the way it is. We're just assessing the roof, right?"

"Yep."

"Then it shouldn't take long. I mean, unless we find something."

"Like what?"

"King Ivy who wants to steal our soul!" he joked, clicking another part of his ladder into place and putting a pin in it.

"I feel like ivy is more feminine than not," she said.

"Fine, fine. Queen Ivy."

Together they hoisted one of the ladders toward the far back wall. Then the other toward the front.

"We can spot-check along all four corners and the back," Vinnie said. "Anything glaring shouldn't be hard to spot."

She was already sweating, and her tee stuck to her back and chest like she'd been hosed down. Her shorts clung to the backs of her thighs, and she reached in her back pocket for an elastic, tying up her hair to get it off her neck before she screamed.

"I need to get a goddamn haircut. Too much hair for all this heat," she growled.

"Do it. Chop it off. It suits you best anyway."

He began to ascend his ladder, she hers.

She didn't know she was going to say it until it came out. "So, how's your mom? I was surprised to hear you didn't take her to chemo the other day. Not that Jace minded, but usually you're so adamant about it."

Vinnie had frozen halfway up his ladder.

She could feel it then, beneath the green overhang of plants and the barn roof, she could feel him trying to weigh it out in his mind. Hurt her or tell her the truth? Remain loyal to his brother or one of his best friends? It was a shitty position to put him in and she suddenly regretted it.

Her foot found the purchase of the next rung.

"She's doing okay. As good as you can while being poisoned, I guess," he said. "I try to be the one to take her. Sometimes things happen, though."

There, she thought, oddly proud of him. He never confirmed he did or didn't take her. Good for you, Vin, she thought.

"I know. That's life."

He sounded disappointed as he said, "Yeah, life can be shitty. Sometimes good people get hurt and that's just not right."

She guessed she was the good people in question and the position his brother had put him in hurt her heart.

CHAPTER 23

IT WAS AMAZING HOW COOL it was up by the vines. The air surrounding them reminded her of the feeling of eating a cucumber or a watermelon in the heat of summer. Somehow, they were always cool. Always refreshing.

On his own ladder, Vinnie was using a hammer from his jean loop to try and part the growth.

"I'll tell you what, this shit is thick as thieves. It's nearly impossible to part." To accent his words, he stabbed with the handle of the hammer toward the ceiling buried beneath the growth. "Thick and tough. You could probably climb a rope made of this stuff."

Bristol was pushing her hands into the ivy because she'd forgotten to bring any kind of tool with her. It was cool to the touch too. But if she pushed far enough—slowly, ever so slowly—she could touch the wooden roof beyond and feel the warmth from the outside.

"This is hardly helping," she said. "I mean, the part I touched isn't compromised in any way, but we can't walk around touching the entirety of the ceiling, now, can we?"

She giggled at the idea. And from the heat of being up so high. Heat rises, indeed, she thought.

"Nope. But we can do a spot check for now. Then let me brainstorm it, yeah?"

"Sure," she said. "Two heads are better than one."

It occurred to her Jace was up in the house working and she was down here in the barn having way more fun with his brother than she had with him in months.

A red flag if ever there was one.

She extended her hand a little farther to the left. Weirded out by the warm and cool contrast of living things and inanimate wood. Creeped out by the hairlike things she thought they called "feet." The part that clung to items so the ivy could secure itself. But also marveling at the ceiling of her barn. *Her* barn. And being up here she realized how much she wanted to stay here. How much she felt this place was hers now. How much she belonged here.

Then Vinnie cursed and yelled "Ouch!" and she turned her head too fast. She lost her footing for a second and felt herself tipping. She had a fearful flash of falling to her death. Or at least to her broken back and a long time in traction. But the ivy around her hand had somehow tightened, or she had gripped it tighter, and it steadied her.

Heart pounding, she managed a squeaky, "Are you okay?" as she righted her feet on the ladder.

"Yeah, just a goddamn monster of a splinter. Ready to move these bitches to the next spot for our highly scientific experiment?"

"You know it," she said and carefully climbed down.

CHAPTER 24

HIS BROTHER AND BRISTOL WERE down in the barn working on their strange project. He had to call Morgan and tell her it was over. He'd made a terrible mistake.

He dialed her number from memory, refusing to put her in his phone as a contact. It rang five times and then he got her voicemail. Sultry, perky voice with a coy ring to it, even digitally.

He'd been a doomed man from the start.

"It's me. We need to talk. Don't call me. I'll call you back soon."

Then he disconnected, realizing what a terrible mistake he'd made.

"We need to talk" is shorthand for "I'm ending things."

Everyone knew that. What a fucking idiot he was.

He made sure his phone was on "Do Not Disturb" mostly because Morgan was not a woman who liked to be told what to do (unless it was in the bedroom). He was fairly certain she'd be at least attempting to call him back.

"Great. Now I can worry about this all day."

Returning to the wonderful world of stocks and investing, he tried to focus his mind on work.

His wife was occupied. He was alone in the house now. And he had time to think. He'd figure it out.

CHAPTER 25

SHE RUBBED HER KNUCKLE AGAINST the leg of her jean shorts. Her fingers had been itching something fierce since she'd been rooting around on the ceiling of the barn. She had a brief wild fear that it was poison ivy she was dealing with but knew from firsthand experience that wasn't true. It was the wrong shape and color. This stuff looked pretty much akin to English Ivy.

The itching was just irritation. Something she'd had most of her life. Dermographism to be exact. When she was a kid she would press bottle caps against her skin over and over to give herself "mermaid scales." The indentations would turn red and rise up and her mother would be furious. But she thought it was pretty.

If this particular bout of it lasted, she'd take Benadryl at bedtime.

"Want to come up to the house for a beer?" she asked.

Vinnie grinned. "You're offering me beer and want to know *if I want it?* That's a trick question, right?"

She shook her head, climbing down carefully. "Can you leave one of these here? We didn't cover nearly enough ground today. Not as much as I thought we would. But I concede, I am hot and tired."

He nodded, wiping his head again with that orange bandana. "Let's move them where you want them now. We're already disgruntled and disgusting."

She snorted. "Okay. Let's do this."

"And you must promise me that you'll be very careful alone. If my stupid brother can't help you, make sure you're being safe. I don't want to get a call that you fell and broke your whole skeleton."

She gave him the Girl Scout promise sign and smiled at him. "On my honor. Promise."

"Don't want anything happening to my favorite sister-in-law."

"I'm your only sister-in-law," she said.

"Still my favorite." Vinnie winked at her and said, "Okay, come on. Let's move these things and go get that beer."

CHAPTER 26

HE WAS DREADING HIS WIFE'S return. As he watched the time, he knew—just *knew*—Morgan was going to call him. Her shift at the bar started soon. She'd be getting his voicemail. She'd be pissed.

And now, to make the stress more stressful, here came Bristol and with her, his brother!

Bristol said she'd talked to Vinnie yesterday. His brother had automatically covered for him. For that he was grateful. But Vin was going to want to talk to him. Scold him. Give him reams of shit.

He was already doing that to himself! He didn't need it from Vin, too.

That internal voice of his that had morals, the angel on his shoulder, scolded that he deserved this. These were the consequences of his actions.

Fuck.

The front door banged open, and Bristol gave him a smile. She was ruddy-faced and sweaty. The hair around her face was damp and stuck to her neck. Her curvy body was covered only with a tank top and jean shorts and her feet were in old Converse sneakers. So old he was pretty sure she'd worn them on their first date.

She'd never looked prettier, and he felt an ache in his heart for what he'd done. His stomach churned from guilt and anxiety.

Next came his brother who gave him a smile too. But this was his brother. They'd been together their whole lives. Jace could read the look in his eyes.

What did you do? Just what the fuck did you do?

Those eyes seemed to burn through him, examining his insides. His soul.

"We're having nice cold beers," Bristol called from the kitchen. "Want one?"

"Uh, sure."

Vin walked past him to get his drink.

When Jace glanced at his phone before following them into the kitchen he saw that he had six missed calls. All from an unmarked contact.

CHAPTER 27

THEY'D HAD SEVERAL BEERS EACH and a pick plate. Cheese, some salami she found still wrapped and sealed in the food box, some nuts. She cracked open a jar of olives and a jar of pickles and then broke open a bag of popcorn.

"Shit, I didn't realize how much shelf-stable food we have," she said.

She was a wee bit tipsy and that was just fine with her. Her fingers itched, she was still sweaty, and inside her, tucked down out of the way was an anger she would be afraid to examine. But she also felt pretty good for some reason.

Vin stopped after a few beers and ate some food. "I've gotta get going soon. I'm going to stop and get Ma her favorite chicken parmigiana sandwich on the way home. See if I can coax her to eat."

"That sounds perfect," Bristol said. "You're such a good son, Vin." She nudged him with her shoulder and saw he was blushing.

"I do try," he said with touching sincerity.

"And you do succeed," she said.

When Vinnie was ready to go, he clapped Jace on the back. "Walk me out, little bro."

"I um—"

"Come on, you've been working from home all day while me and Bristol dangled from ladders down there in the heat. Getting up off your ass will be good for you."

He said it all with a big smile on his face, but Bristol knew Vinnie well enough, had been close to him long enough, that she could detect the teeth and claws under the statement.

Vin wanted to talk to his brother alone. And that made her immensely happy. Maybe he'd punch him in the neck while he was at it.

She scratched her knuckle constantly, worrying the same spot. It was driving her nuts. She'd have to clean it well. Maybe douse it with some peroxide.

Jace got up from the table like he was going to the guillotine. All through the chat he'd been patting his pocket obsessively. The one that contained his phone, no doubt. Anticipation or worry? She didn't know.

She watched him shuffle off as if to his execution.

Hoping Vin lit into his brother good, she stood and cleared the table. She could go for a long hot shower, maybe a glass of wine once the beer buzz fled, and a good book. She had a whole box of them next to the bed. A good folk horror seemed to be in order, she thought. Given their current location.

"Don't freak yourself out," she muttered.

But it didn't seem possible. Despite everything, she was starting to feel strong. Nearly indestructible somehow.

CHAPTER 28

"YOU WANT TO TELL ME exactly what the fuck you're doing?"

"What do you mean?" Jace swallowed hard. It was obvious no amount of playing dumb was going to work.

"Why did Bristol inform me that I was busy, and *you* took Ma to chemo the other day? I'm pretty sure it was my ass in that seat getting her saltines and Gatorade."

"Look I—"

"And it's not even that you lied about that. It's the fact that if you're lying it's because you're fucking over that wife of yours again. Hear me? *Again.*"

"I had something to take care of is all," Jace stammered.

"Sure you did. Something you couldn't tell Bristol? Or me? Or Ma? And so you dragged us into it. She's no fool. She may be sick but she's still there, Jace. She knows you lied, and she knows what that means."

"Bristol and I are having some issues—"

"So you cheat!"

Vin's voice was so loud and ringing it made Jace flinch. "Can you keep it down please?"

"Oh, so there is a reason to keep it quiet. Perhaps the reason being you're fucking around on your wife? Once a cheater, always a cheater." Vin leaned in, teeth bared.

He was furious and Jace took a step back, expecting his brother to swing on him.

"That woman already forgave you once. As usual, it's you, the idiot who falls ass backward into a good thing and then proceeds to stomp all over it with your big emotions and your big needs."

"She's not sure she wants a baby anymore!" Jace blurted.

"So what? So the fuck what? I'm sure that's upsetting but this is your solution? To take your toys and run away. To do something irrevocably awful to your partner? What's wrong with you?"

Jace opened his mouth, then closed it again.

"I can answer that for you, little brother. You're a spoiled rotten brat."

"Look, I made a mistake. And I'm rectifying it. I called Morgan and told her I can't—"

"Shut up. Shut the fuck up. I don't want to know any more than I have to. I don't want to be a party to this. If she doesn't want a baby, there's a reason, no doubt. It's either too hard for her physically, emotionally, or mentally. Or all three! Have you tried helping her? Or just pouting because things aren't going your way?"

Jace bristled at that. "This is none of your business."

"It became my goddamn business when you used me and our fucking mother as an alibi! If you ever do anything like this again, I won't cover for you. And neither will Ma. We talked about it. And we decided something else."

"What's that?" Jace growled.

"That Bristol deserves our loyalty way more than you do."

CHAPTER 29

THE SHOWER WAS LUXURIOUS. JUST what she needed. Steaming hot water beat down over her sore back muscles. Her shoulders still ached from working overhead so much. She shivered briefly under the heat of the shower. Her body suddenly haywire, unsure of whether the water was hot or cold.

Bristol shut her eyes, letting the water run over her head and face. She soaped up slowly and hissed when she felt the sting of soap against her irritated knuckles. Next time they went up she'd have to wear gloves.

Washing her hair slowly, she tried to imagine what Vinnie was saying to his brother. Nothing good, she was sure. Vinnie was no fool and he'd been roped into Jace's lies. One thing she knew about Vinnie was he didn't like to be sucked into other people's drama and bullshit. And lying to someone you were supposed to love ticked both of those boxes and then some.

"I hope he beats his ass," she whispered and sighed.

What a fucking mess.

She rubbed her belly realizing, for all intents and purposes, it was the sole root of this issue. Maybe not the outside but definitely what lay beneath. Her uterus was what he had an issue with. The fact that it was empty of their child. And she hated him for it.

She realized then she hated him a little more each day and it hurt her all the way down to her core.

Outside the shower she took her time, in no hurry to get back to the awkwardness that was her relationship with Jace right now. She pulled her hair into a wet knot atop her head and slathered on lotion, once more wincing from the stinging on her knuckles.

Finding her cheaters, she shoved them on and examined her skin. Just there above her middle knuckle was a small black dot poking out from her skin.

"Splinter," she sighed. "Have to be more careful rooting around in there, you dummy."

The tweezers weren't where they normally were, so she had to dig around in the steamy bathroom. When she finally found them, she sat on the toilet lid and got hold of the tiny black dot with the sharp ends.

When she pulled, it tugged her skin enough that she could see it move.

"Ouch, goddamn. I didn't know ivy could give you splinters." Then she remembered she had been digging around by the roof. "But wood will."

Another tug and there was an intense tearing sensation beneath her skin.

"Jesus."

She pulled just a bit harder, keeping steady pressure on the tweezers.

Another ripping, tugging sensation and the thing pulled free. A little.

"What the fuck?"

Disgust and a small flash of horror flooded her as she pulled. And pulled.

When all was said and done, about two inches of blackish-green vine pulled free from her skin.

She swallowed hard to keep from gagging.

"No wonder it stung." A slightly hysterical laugh escaped her, and she clapped a hand over her mouth.

Running her fingertip up the length of that knuckle, she palpated it to see if any vine remained farther up beneath the skin.

It didn't seem to and yet she worried it was in there. Lurking. How had she not felt that go in? How had she failed to realize how big it was?

She shook from head to toe like a dog. "Shake it off. Weird. Creepy. Gross. But definitely not fatal."

She doused her hand in peroxide, watching—fascinated—as it fizzed up repeatedly.

Dippity insisted on helping her—aka jumping on her—when she rooted through the bottom of the linen closet for the first aid kit.

A glob of antibiotic ointment and a large Band-Aid later she was good as new. Sort of. She was still a little grossed out.

Bristol pointed a finger at the dog who did his best circus routine, sitting on his haunches, swinging his front paws in the air fetchingly.

"Next time . . . gloves."

CHAPTER 30

THINGS HAD BEEN EVEN WEIRDER when Jace came inside. She went to pour herself a glass of wine. Jace looked surprised when she entered without offering him one.

So, she poked him.

"Everything okay with your brother? You two aren't fighting, are you?"

She smiled.

He blanched.

"No. Not at all. He just wanted to talk about Mom."

"I should call her." She patted her legging pocket as if to find her phone.

Somehow watching him squirm was even better today than yesterday. Yesterday, she'd even felt a little sympathy for him. Today, no such thing existed. Her anger and hurt were winning today.

"It's kind of late, don't you think."

"Well, only eight o'clock but . . ."

"Chemo," he added helpfully. And hopefully, she noted.

"Yes, that's true. I can wait. She knows I'm here if she needs me."

"Of course."

He was so on edge he literally hovered on the edge of his seat, which was why she was utterly shocked and amazed when he got up and went upstairs without his phone.

Stupid him. Lucky her.

She heard the toilet seat lid and smiled. Most likely, as was often his M.O., he worked himself up to the point his stomach was upset. And now, he was realizing he forgot his phone, which would probably leave him there longer.

"I hope you shit yourself inside out," she muttered, picking up his phone.

She immediately turned off "Do Not Disturb" and punched in his passcode. The phone informed her that was the wrong passcode.

"Interesting."

She looked at the notifications and saw they were all from a generic number. About sixteen of them.

She laughed and took a photo of his phone with hers.

Snagging her wine, she walked out onto the porch, sat on the old swing she had every intention of refinishing, and dialed the number.

It only took four rings and the line was answered.

"Hello?"

Hesitant. Suspicious. Plus, Bristol thought, who answers an unknown number nowadays? No one. This woman had to have some idea.

"Hello, to whom am I speaking?" Bristol said calmly.

"Morgan," the woman said and Bristol literally heard her gulp.

She realized that was a mistake.

"Thanks." Bristol hung up before going back inside.

~

When Jace returned to the living room she'd returned his phone to the end table but put it a few inches to the left. She had also left "Do Not Disturb" off so the phone was now a constant barrage of vibrations.

He paled and looked up at her.

Bristol cocked an eyebrow. "Sounds like someone really needs to talk to you."

He stared at her, studying her face she made sure to keep calm and neutral.

It started to buzz yet again, and she stood. "You should get that." Deciding she had liked it better outside, she took her wine glass and walked out onto the porch.

She sat watching fireflies and listening to the crickets. Somehow, she was quickly adapting to the sights, sounds, and smells of the country. If you'd asked her a week ago, she'd never have thought she could adapt so fast.

Turned out she really loved it here.

As she listened to the night deepening around her, she scratched absently at her knuckles.

CHAPTER 31

"STOP CALLING ME!"

"You called me and left some cryptic ass message."

"I'm sorry. I should have thought that through better, but things are weird. Here."

Morgan laughed. "We need to talk. Everyone knows what that means. Why even leave a message if you didn't want me to call. Just call back!"

"I don't know! I told you I wasn't thinking. Look, this was all a mistake. And I'm in the wrong. It was my fault. I never should have taken you up on—"

"Oh no, you instigated this. You didn't take me up on shit. You. Called. Me. You propositioned me. You were the initiator."

"True. Absolutely true. You're right. I'm sorry. I made a terrible mistake."

"She knows," she said, and he detected a bit of venom in her voice.

"She suspects."

"No. She knows."

"There's no way she can know for sure—"

"Well, she called me."

Ice ran through his veins. "No."

"Yes. Is this her?" Morgan proceeded to read off Bristol's phone number.

He was currently hiding in the main bathroom. His legs went so weak he had to sit on the toilet seat. He was very close to having to empty his bowels all over again.

"What did she say?" he breathed.

"Why should I tell you? You're breaking up with me!"

"There's nothing to break up. We fucked. Once."

He thought she sniffled but realized she was laughing. "And it wasn't that impressive. I'll do what I want. Call when I want. Who I want. I have her number. Maybe I'll call her, and we can have a nice little chat."

"Don't you dare."

"Or what? What the fuck are you going to do, *Jace?*"

He gritted his teeth so hard they creaked.

"For starters, Bruce and I are great friends. Maybe he doesn't need you as a bartender. Maybe he needs someone younger and hotter and not as rude to customers."

"Fuck off," she said but sounded unsure. She made good money at the Piano Key. Great money, in fact. He knew that for certain.

"Try me and see if I don't," he said.

Then he was listening to dead air because the woman who seemed like the perfect way to blow off steam a mere 48 hours ago now seemed like the ninth circle of hell.

CHAPTER 32

SHE FELT DEHYDRATED AFTER A single glass of wine so she put her head over the sink and put cold washcloths on the back of her neck. It was something her mother used to do when she was a kid, and it soothed her.

Her head hurt a bit. Her heart also. But not as much as it had. She'd made a decision for her well-being—both mental and physical—and her husband's response was to cheat on her. Almost immediately.

That spoke volumes about him and said nothing about her. There hadn't even been any more discussions. Any offers of support or help. Just making a phone call to arrange cheating on her. For the second time in their fairly short marriage.

"Done," she said. It needed no elaboration.

She'd have to talk to her editor about an advance for *Watching Fireflies*, her next kids' book, when she returned to her deadlines the following week. If she could buy out Jace's share of the house, she could have it to herself. Maybe cash out the 401k from her former office job. She might even have to go back to traditional work. But she would if she had to. She'd figure it out.

The dog circled her legs, panting.

"It is a little hot, buddy," she murmured. "Mommy will turn the air down in a moment." And then, looking down at his face, she said, "We could turn the barn into a venue. Rent it out for weddings and family reunions. I bet Vin would help me with that. I could live here and work here and have a side gig here. I just need to get rid of the dead weight."

It took everything in her to finally climb into bed with him. He was lying on his side, his face averted, and they'd been married long enough for Bristol to know when her husband was playing possum. Which he definitely was at the moment.

He didn't want to engage with her and that was fine.

For a moment in the dark, she realized how swiftly things had dissolved once they arrived here. And how it wasn't as upsetting to her as she would have anticipated.

She listened to Dippity rustling around in his bed, trying to get comfortable. When he finally settled, she realized she was dropping off to sleep. It wasn't much later that he woke her with his fervent barking. At her.

CHAPTER 33

THE DREAM WAS TO BLAME. Here, out in the wilds near the barn. Everything growing in a riotous manner now the weather had turned hot and humid. That was all it took for foliage to take off and grow out of control.

Her machete had hacked through all kinds of weeds and growth. Low hanging tree limbs and debris. If she could clear the barn of its extra growth she could start prepping it for her venue idea.

Just her and the property. The forest and the barn. Living symbiotically. A good life. A simple life. Just what she'd always wanted.

But there were thick invasive vines that were not the pretty ones she now cultivated for the roof of the barn.

These were thick and brown with minimal green growth. As thick around as her wrist. Some even thicker.

The machete had no power over them. But maybe if she could get hold of the bigger ones and yank them free. Then she could drag them away.

She wrapped her hands around them, squeezing and pulling with all her might. The vines reacted, surprising her. A jerking swaying motion that made it hard to hold and keep her grip.

Somewhere the dog was barking. Really going nuts over something. Probably a squirrel or a rabbit.

She squeezed, yanked, tore at the thick, harsh wood beneath her hands, feeling it buck and sway in response. Bristol leaned into it, grunting with the effort. If she could take care of this, everything would be fine. Everything would be good. Life could carry on as it should. No more sadness. No more pain.

Then something was tugging at her, pulling. The barking was louder. More insistent. And whatever was attached to her shook and strained. Finally breaking her concentration and pulling her focus from the vines.

Then a hand smacked at her face and she was suddenly falling.

Falling off Jace's chest. Her hands, the ones wrapped around his neck, loosening as she slid to the side.

"Jesus Christ, Bristol!" he wheezed. "You were fucking choking me to death!"

She noticed two things. She was smiling. And her hands were itching something fierce.

CHAPTER 34

"WHAT THE FUCK?" HE CROAKED.

She hadn't said anything. Just gone to get him some ice packs from the freezer, having to stop twice for giggling fits. Hand shoved against her mouth, body shaking, eyes leaking tears of mirth. It wasn't fucking funny, but my god, it actually was.

What's that about instant karma?

The only thing was poor Dippity. He eyed her warily as she walked through the house and Bristol hated that.

"Don't look at me like that, Dippity Do," she said. "It was an accident. Mommy had a bad dream."

But had it been? Bad? More like powerful, empowering, determined.

Either way, it had just been a dream and Jace would be fine. Call it penance for running out on her the moment she didn't do exactly what he wanted.

He took the ice packs and wrapped them around his throat. Before she laid them on, she saw pink marks darkening to plum in some spots on his neck. She had to press her forearm to her mouth to keep from laughing.

"Are you okay?" she managed, realizing she didn't much care. But there were social mores to be observed. At least for the time being.

"No, I'm not fucking okay."

Rage, hot and liquid, surged through her and she found herself bent over him as he lay there prone in the bed. Holding ice packs to his throat that bore her handprints. His eyes went wide and, surprisingly, behind her, Dippity growled.

"Good. Neither am I, you cheating twerp."

She didn't think his eyes could go wider and yet they did. "I didn't—"

"Oh, come the fuck on. Are you really going to lie on top of everything you've done?"

She leaned in a little closer and watched him literally push his body back into the mattress as if to get away from her if he could.

"Would you like me to call Morgan to come get you? Take you home? Tend to your wounds? Is she going to have your baby? Are you so close you're going to make a person together? Is that the goal? Just to have a person you can claim?"

"It was a mistake."

She leaned in so close their noses were nearly touching. Had they been on good terms it might have been intimate, sexy even.

In the moment, it rang of threat.

"You were a mistake, Jace. I never should have given you a second chance after you showed me who you really were. Your true colors." She pushed a finger against his chest. "But mistakes can be rectified, can't they."

"Hold on, Bristol. I love you. I fucked up."

"Oh, so many times. The moment I didn't give you what you wanted you went running back out again. Running to the first available and willing pussy to take in your poor disgruntled cock."

She pressed her mouth against his ear as she spoke, and he flinched.

"I am done with you. I'm going to figure out how to get you out of here. And then I'm going to go on with my life as if you never fucking existed."

"Bristol, please, just take some time to think about it. We can fix this. *I can fix this.*"

She stood, turned on her heels, and walked out of the room.

Down on the sofa, she lay there thinking about the barn and her possible business and a life without Jace weighing her down. She scratched her knuckles, promising herself in the morning when she wasn't so tired she'd examine them again and give them another good cleaning.

"Come on, Dippy boy," she said to the dog.

He sat at the foot of the sofa and whined. But he declined her offer of snuggles.

CHAPTER 35

THURSDAY

THE NEXT MORNING JACE WAS gone with a note that said: *Gone to the city. Doc appointment. Can we please talk this over? I have to stop in the office before I come back. Call and check in ANY TIME. I love you . . .*

Call and check in any time. She snorted. "Too little, too late."

If he wasn't with Morgan, it was because she hadn't wanted him, most likely. The longer this whole thing went on, the more she realized her husband was a spineless simpleton. Had he always been that way, or had she just woken up?

Coffee seemed too hot for some reason. Maybe the temperature. So, Bristol mixed up a cup of instant, not even bringing the water to a boil, simply added warm water to the powder. A little sugar, the smallest dollop of milk, and she sighed with her first sip.

She fed the dog who, she noticed, was still keeping a distance from her. He wasn't aggressive but did appear wary.

"You strangle one husband in your sleep and it's the cold shoulder from you, is it?"

She laughed lightly. The situation wasn't funny. She knew she shouldn't find it funny. And yet she did.

Food was unappealing so she wandered out on the back porch in her nightshirt. She sat on the steps where it seemed like years ago they'd eaten a chicken dinner and watched the dog play. Had that only been a few days ago? Time was weird. Life was weird. And in the life department, marriage was weird.

Bristol tilted her head back to the sun and drank it in. Normally this kind of heat bothered her, but she was in the country now. Maybe that made all the difference. Not surrounded by macadam and blaring car horns and tall buildings. Maybe being out here with trees and nature all around changed the whole experience.

She sipped her coffee and mulled over what to do about her husband.

"I suppose burying him in the woods is out of the question."

She suppressed another laugh but was surprised to find a small part of her instinct had responded with a hearty:

No, that's not out of the question.

Dippity had appeared at the top step, regarding her with caution. "Are you really that afraid of me now?" She reached for him.

Years of being his mistress conditioned him so he stayed where he was, but she could see his tail was tucked between his short little legs and he was shaking more than normal.

"Dip, buddy, Mommy would never hurt you."

She stroked the top of his head, and he stayed stock still as if frozen in fear. When she pulled her hand back, he sniffed it. His lunatic, frantic dachshund sniffs, as if he could inhale the entire item to determine what it was and if it was safe or edible.

He sniffed harder and gave a low growl as he backed up.

Surprised yet again, Bristol examined her hand and laughed. "You're afraid of a splinter, doggy-doo? I guess I didn't get it all. I'll go fix that now and you can stop growling at me, you ferocious beast."

As she ascended the steps, he bolted past her into the yard. Jace she could handle, but she couldn't stand having her dog upset with her.

~

This time it fucking hurt. Bad. She stood in the bathroom beneath

86

the bright overheads with the makeup mirrors flipped on as well and tugged the small visible end with the tweezers. Every pull there was an intense tearing sensation. A tugging so deep she feared it would rip all her meat out.

"Jesus fucking Christ," she grunted, sweating. Her body slick with the cold slime of pain. "What the hell?"

She pulled and managed only about a sixteenth of an inch extraction. She pulled again and had to stop lest she gag. She could see beneath the skin, from her middle knuckle to where her top knuckle joined her hand. A lump ran the entire length. Was there really a splinter of vine in there that long? That it went from mid-finger to her hand? My God, how had she missed that?

She had no idea. What she did know was it hurt like a motherfucker and made her want to lie down and cry.

Giving one more halfhearted tug, she extracted just a bit more. Her body trembled, her stomach heaved. That coffee was going to come back up if she wasn't careful.

"I'll have to do more later. Maybe make my own doctor appointment in the city."

She surveyed the half inch or so of dark matter sticking out of her finger and watched, amazed, as it began to withdraw back into her skin. Bristol didn't think, she simply grabbed the nail clippers and clipped off the end.

Then she threw her head back and screamed. Her knees buckled, dumping her to the bathroom floor.

CHAPTER 36

SHE HAD NO IDEA HOW long she lay there. When she awoke, the sweat had dried and her hand was just a dull throb as opposed to white hot fire.

The dog watched her warily, wagging his tail nervously, dancing in place as if he wanted to approach her but was afraid.

"Come here, buddy," she rasped.

He did then. Inching closer and closer before finally licking her face and whining.

"I'm okay. I'm fine. I just . . ."

Just what? Fainted? Passed out? Hit the ground like a sack of rocks?

"Fell down," she finished.

She slowly got to her feet, gripping the vanity for stability. Her head throbbed along with her hand, and she groaned.

"Jesus fucking Christ. I feel like I'm a thousand."

Filling a cup from the sink with cold water, she drank it down quickly. It helped, so she drank another.

In her mind's eye, the barn flashed bright and cool and comforting. She could go out there while Jace was gone and scope out the space. Start brainstorming. And then she could talk to Vin the next time they saw each other. Get his take on it. Taking action would do her good. She'd feel better with a mission.

She changed into old sneakers, a tank, and over it a wrecked, loose sundress she used for puttering around the house and yard when it was hot. In the bathroom, she took the antibacterial ointment and slathered it on the open wound thickly. For a moment the world seemed to swell and shrink. The pain was hot and intense all over again. She took small sips of air until the sensation passed and then found two large knuckle bandages. She wrapped the wound with one and then mounted the second over the top knuckle and the bandage on her finger. "Sloppy but effective."

Then she took the steps slowly. She felt better at the bottom and headed into the kitchen.

Rooting through moving boxes, she found an aluminum water bottle and filled it with cold tap water. Then she whistled for Dippity.

"Come on, munchkin. Let's go to the barn."

She heard him stir but he didn't appear.

"Walk!" she tried again.

She could hear his tail beating rhythmically against the wall but he still didn't appear.

"Last call for a *wa–aaaaa–llllllk*."

Nothing.

"Suit yourself," she said.

She made sure he had a chew and some water and then locked the door behind her.

The closer she got to the barn, the better she felt.

~

Her intention had been to just look today. She already bore wounds from her last ceiling encounter in the barn, and yet, the closer she got the more fixated she became on what lurked at the top of the barn.

Getting close to the end of the trail leading to the barn, she noted the vines were farther along than they had been.

She walked up to it, studying the dark green leaves and thick vines. They'd crawled past where they had been when she'd first seen the spot.

"Do you creep when the weather gets warm?" she said playfully. Then felt silly talking to plants.

Although, her grandmother had always sworn that made them grow. She remembered a science teacher saying it was simply when you talked to them you were breathing carbon dioxide all over them, which is what they needed to grow. Either way, she was chatting with vegetation.

Close by something rustled. She knew there was no way it was the plant, had to be a bird in the brush or a squirrel or something even smaller. Though once again she noticed the absence of forest sounds beyond this point.

Surely it was her presence and nothing more.

Inside the barn she put her water bottle and tote down and shook Vinnie's tall metal ladders one at a time. Still sturdy. They weren't going to buckle and dump her on her ass. Thank goodness.

"I'll be extra careful and not look down," she mumbled.

Taking the steps slowly, she got to the top and studied the dense green vegetation before her. Dark green. Thick. Strong. The smell of it was neutral. Just green and alive. That's all.

She found herself stroking a leaf and liking the smooth but pulpy feel. Then she plunged her hand, the injured one no less, into the dense growth and pushed toward the wooden roof beyond. She was in past her wrist before her fingertips touched wood. Solid wood. Not spongy or pulpy.

"That's good. Need a solid roof for an event venue. Can't be leaking on the patrons."

She stretched her hand to the right, feeling nothing but solid wood. Pushing her hand in every direction, going as far as she could, she found the ceiling in good condition.

Descending a step, she tried to pull her hand free and was met with a bit of resistance. No pain. It was just a struggle to get free. She was stuck on something. Finally, pulling hard, she felt the ladder wobble as she managed to get her hand free.

Her naked hand.

Bristol shook her head. "You stole my bandage!"

At the bottom of the steps, she examined her wounds. Still open, still red, still puffy, but she hadn't brought any additional bandages with her so she'd have to be careful.

"It's fine. I can clean it up later."

And up the other ladder she went. Repeating her palpations of the ceiling. Studying what she could see, hoping she didn't find any issues. She was really fixated on her business idea now and excitement had set up residence in her belly.

One of the vines tightened around her wrist and she flinched. It relaxed a bit and so did she. There was a rustling and what she could only describe as a wave of movement through the lush ceiling. She watched, mesmerized, as it happened. Then the vine was tight around her again just as she lost her balance, one foot swinging free of the ladder.

Her other hand gripped the top of the ladder, the this-is-not-a-step step and the whole ladder shook.

"Fuck."

The vine, tight around her arm, steadied her as she worked her foot back over and found her balance again.

Only then did it release enough for her to withdraw her hand. Around her pinky was twined the tiniest baby vine. So small and pale green it looked like a piece of jewelry.

She watched it as it waved slightly, curling around her finger.

Then she realized Dippity was barking his ass off at the house. His warnings were so loud it carried all the way down the trail. With dachshunds you got a lot of bark for your buck. They often sounded like much bigger dogs. And right now, he did.

That was his someone is here bark, she realized, forgetting about the vines for the moment.

Who was here? Dippity wouldn't bark at Jace like that. So, who was on her property? Who had come to her home?

CHAPTER 37

"DIPPITY! DIPPITY!" SHE HISSED AS she approached. "What is all the racket?"

Only her car was parked in front of the house. That didn't mean someone wasn't here. It would be easy enough to park halfway down the drive and walk up.

This thought was confirmed when a dark-haired woman stomped from around the back of the house. She stopped dead in her tracks when she saw Bristol.

Tank top, cut off shorts, overworn Vans. Big boobs, bright blue eyes, curvy in all the right places.

"Hello, Morgan," Bristol said, tucking her hands into her pockets. She winced briefly from the friction on her wounds.

The other woman blinked, drew back a little, but then smiled. "Mrs. Stokes," she said.

"Oh, please. We share a cock. Call me Bristol."

Again, the woman flinched, and it made Bristol's heart glad. Absently, she rubbed her hand up and down within the confines of her pocket to scratch that now nearly constant itch.

"You okay?" Morgan said, indicating the motion.

"Don't you worry about me. What can I do for you? If you're looking for your boyfriend, he's not here. He's at the doctor in the city. Had a little boo-boo." Bristol drew the two words out in a pouty voice like a child.

"I thought we could talk like adults." Morgan looked unsure of herself.

"Well, one of us can at least," Bristol said.

When she took a step forward the other woman took a step back.

From the direction of the barn, she heard a soft, shushing-swishing sound. She cocked her head to listen.

"I just wanted to talk to you about Jace. And what happened."

"Not here to apologize, then?"

"Well, no. I figure if anyone should apologize for us, it's him. I'm not married. He is. It's his wrong on you. Not mine."

"But you knew he was married."

She inclined her head, having the good grace to blush a little. "A bit unhappily, to hear him talk about it," she said.

Bristol laughed. "Of course. Poor man with a terrible wife. Always the victim, that one. Did he happen to tell you he cheated on me before? That you're not the first." She leaned forward and relished the sudden look of alarm on Morgan's face. "Which means, you, my dear, are not special. Not at all. You're a warm body, a willing cunt, and dumb enough to fall for it."

That did it. The woman snarled at her.

Inside, the dog barked. In her pocket, her hand itched. In her head, she heard the shushing and swishing. She was sweating and the sun beat down on her. Only June but at least ninety out in the open under the beating sun.

And then she was calm.

"That wasn't very fair of me, was it?"

Morgan's movement was arrested by surprise. "What?"

"It wasn't fair of me. It's him who's married, like you said. It was his action to proceed with or stop. And he chose to proceed. That's on him. Not me and not you. I'm taking a walk out to the barn. Would you like to see it? I think I'm going to rent it out for events. You know, when I divorce Jace. He's all yours if you want him."

The woman blinked, swallowed, and for whatever reason, decided to follow her lover's wife into the woods.

CHAPTER 38

SHE LET MORGAN WALK BEHIND her as she led her down the path.

"I can't believe I'm walking down a path into the woods with Jace's wife."

"I can't believe I'm showing you my dream!" Bristol said, laughing. "But I guess, in the end, us girls have to stick together."

As they approached the barn the coolness increased, the thick lush feel of humid air, the whispering, shushing, sliding sound became more prevalent.

At least to Bristol it did.

Morgan appeared to be fixated on the looming barn.

"That thing is enormous."

"It is," Bristol agreed, "But that's not even the best part."

Again, the absence of bird cries or animals moving in the underbrush. Her fingers, still shoved in her pockets, itched and tingled.

With a toss of her head to indicate the other woman should follow, she walked into the barn.

Morgan followed and immediately looked up. "Holy shit," she said.

For that moment it seemed she'd forgotten where she was and who she was with. The thick canopy of green growth had that effect.

"Pretty impressive right?" Bristol said.

"I've never seen anything like it," she said.

"Neither had I until this place."

Together the women looked up and peered again. Head cocked, Bristol could still hear the sliding, whispery sounds.

She closed her eyes, swaying slightly, letting her body, the organism, the whole, take in what she was experiencing.

She opened her eyes and smiled. "It wraps around. Outside. It's amazing, you should see it."

It seemed Morgan's body, her organism, her whole, was also hearing or feeling something because she nodded as if slightly drunk. Then she followed Bristol outside to the place she'd noted new growth.

"The whole back and down to here at this point. I think it'll grow more with the weather. Now that it's hot."

Morgan nodded, stepping closer to where the riotous tangles of green ropey vines had encircled a small tree. When she was close enough to reach, Bristol shoved her.

It came as second nature. The tiny vine still clinging to her pinkie had already weaved its way around the digit. The vine inside her knuckle seemed to vibrate and twitch.

She laughed a wild short bark of surprise. Had she known she would do that? Why had she done that? What the fuck was going on?

But also, under it all, she was very calm. Very serene. It would all be okay. Morgan would be taken care of.

And as she watched, it had already begun. The vines strayed over the floundering woman. Some of the larger ones encircled her wrists. Some wound around her legs. She opened her mouth to scream and a few smaller ones, acting as a unit, took the chance to dive right in.

Bristol watched—on one level horrified, on another charmed. What a gorgeous thing it was to witness—the unity. It had been so long since she'd felt united with anything or anyone. Maybe when she had carried her child very briefly before losing her.

Somehow, she knew it had been a girl.

This was akin to that. Life, symbiosis, the beauty of nature.

In her cheeks, heat burned. The heat and burn in her infected hand matched. She watched as the vines covered and disabled the woman who'd seen fit to fuck her husband.

How long would Morgan be aware of what was happening? Bristol had no idea. And she didn't really care. Nature had a way of taking care of problems.

Bristol went back to her examination of the roof. Whistling and swaying as she probed the wood above her head. As the vines caressed her and seemed to stir around her, she smiled. A few times she felt a sharp twinge like a needle prick but carried on. It would all be fine. Suddenly, she simply believed everything would turn out fine.

CHAPTER 39

"WHAT HAPPENED HERE?" DOC CARLISLE asked.

"Sleep accident."

The old man cocked an eyebrow. "What happened in your sleep that left handprints on your throat, Jace?"

Carlisle had been his doc since he was a kid. Now he looked the man in the eye and said, "My wife had night terrors. It was a thing. And it was an accident."

Carlisle nodded. "You sure?"

"Absolutely."

"Okay. I'll say this, sadly there's not a whole hell of a lot we can do about bruises. Any trouble breathing?"

"Nope."

"Swallowing?"

"Nope."

"Open up."

Jace did as asked, and the doc grunted softly. "Everything looks okay. This isn't a regular occurrence, is it?"

"No. It's the first and only time it's ever happened."

"Good. If it continues, I'd look into a sleep specialist for your wife. Maybe a sleep study will help get to the root of it. Any significant stressors in your life and hers?"

"Trying to have a baby," Jace said softly. Up until recently it hadn't been a lie.

Carlisle clapped him on the shoulder. "That's enough to stress anyone out. I wish you luck. Now let's get a look at that weight while I have you . . ."

CHAPTER 40

IT WASN'T UNTIL HE WAS out in the daylight that he had reception again. The behemoth of an office building Doc Carlisle was in left him with no bars. Given the fact he'd waited nearly an hour to be seen and had been in with the doc half of that and had to do the checkout process, he was two hours behind on his notifications. Now his phone was full of messages.

TEXT ME OR I'M CALLING YOUR WIFE

TEXT ME OR YOU'LL BE SORRY

PLEASE TEXT ME

YOU KNOW WHAT? FUCK YOU. TEXT ME OR I'M GOING TO SEE YOUR WIFE, ASSHOLE

THAT'S IT. I'M ON MY WAY TO SAY HI TO YOUR MISSES.

I'M HERE AT YOUR MAILBOX. (With that one there was a photo and it was, indeed, his mailbox).

I'M GOING UP. YOU CAN GO TO HELL, ASSHOLE

And then they stopped. Somehow, for Jace, the silence was worse.

He scrolled, looking for any messages from Bristol, and found none. He didn't know if that was good or bad.

His stomach churned and he had a moment where he feared he might shit himself right there on the sidewalk. Then the wave of nausea and cramping passed, and he was trembling in the hot June sun like it was twenty degrees.

"Jesus fucking Christ," he said.

In his car, he sat, debating whether to call home or pretend he had no idea. Maybe Morgan had changed her mind. Maybe she'd been bluffing.

He went to the nearest bar and sat in the cool dark and drank three beers for courage. Beer and bars were what had gotten him into this mess, but he didn't know what else to do.

CHAPTER 41

SHE WAS VERY CALM, AND part of Bristol knew that wasn't necessarily a good thing. It was, however, how she felt.

Shoving her hands into the vines, she managed to find Morgan's pocket and pushed her hand in. She found her keys and her phone and withdrew.

"You won't be needing these," she said.

The shrouded figure writhed and tossed and gave a muffled cry but couldn't break free.

"Don't worry. It won't be long now," Bristol said. "At least, I don't think it will. I've never actually done this before."

She walked back toward the main house and the driveway, moving slowly and sinuously in the high hot sun. Her body moved as if she heard some inaudible music. A sound only for her. The soft cool sound of growth and creeping.

She found the SUV down by their mailbox and climbed in. She

drove the car up to the house and turned it toward the path out to the barn. It was tight, the trees reaching out to slap and scratch the side of the car. When she finally reached the clearing, she sat for a moment, listening. Then drove past the barn, past the tree where she'd fallen asleep and into the thickness of the trees. There was just enough space for her to eke through and then she hit an open spot with nothing but dead leaves and some overgrown bushes.

The car, a lovely hunter green, would hopefully blend in.

Backtracking, she stood by the barn and studied the place where she knew the car was. Bristol was glad to see she couldn't find it even if she stared. Come fall that might change but fall was still far away. No time to worry about that now.

She turned off location settings, turned on airplane mode, took out the SIM card, snapped it in half, and dropped it in her bottle of water. Lastly, she stomped on the phone until it was in pieces. Some combination of those things would simply have to work, she hoped.

It was worth a try.

She climbed the second ladder, the one she hadn't gotten to, and went back to examining the ceiling. Imagining her new dream. Tables below lit with lanterns filled with flickering pillar candles. People drinking wine, laughing, talking. Above, the lush, cool canopy of vines watching over them.

The perfect setting. A wonderful dream.

CHAPTER 42

JACE LET OUT A LONG low breath as he rounded the corner and spotted his mailbox. No car parked near it.

Halfway up the drive, still nothing. Parked outside his home, still nothing. Of course, that didn't mean Morgan hadn't already come and gone.

Inside the house the dog was going absolutely apeshit. A bad sign.

Jace didn't need his key, the door was unlocked. He pushed in and hushed the dachshund who leapt at him. Jace managed to catch him in midair. The dog was trembling. Not like a small dog's constant tremble but like a creature that's freaked out.

"What's wrong, Dippity Do? Where's Mommy?"

At the word "mommy" the dog stopped barking but the shaking continued.

"Bristol!" he shouted into the dim depths of the house. The outside brightness served to make the house's interior appear darker than it probably was. "Bris! Are you here?"

She was mad at him. Furious even. But there's no way she'd take it out on Dippity by neglecting him. She must have gone out. The problem was her car was parked right out front.

For a split second he had a sudden panicked worry Morgan had come and abducted his wife. It would explain Bristol's car being here and Morgan's being gone.

"Or she just never came and was threatening you to scare you." He rubbed his head. "Or she came and Bristol went off on her." His stomach rolled. "Don't go jumping to conclusions for fuck's sake," he muttered.

Dippity thought he was talking to him and began to furiously lick Jace's face. Laughing despite the situation, he set the dog on the floor. Dippity immediately darted out the front door into the brilliant sun. Running like his life was in danger, he barreled down the path toward the barn with Jace chasing behind him, calling his name.

CHAPTER 43

SHE HEARD HIM COMING BUT didn't stop what she was doing. Let him come. Let him see. He was the reason this whole thing had started. He was the reason she had sought the comfort of the woods. But Bristol thought maybe she should thank him. He was the reason she was no longer alone and floundering.

When he rounded the corner, she was hanging in the dead center of the barn, supported by the vines that had twined around her hands, wrists, and forearms.

"Jesus, Bristol! Are you okay? Let me get you—"

She laughed, swinging her legs and advancing a few more feet like a kid on playground monkey bars.

When she first realized the vines that had twined around her pinky earlier had embedded themselves in the top layer of flesh, she had panicked. Fear had spiked hot and sudden in her stomach. But then, as she watched it encircle her pinky, move up her arm, the very tip

waving as if in a breeze, she calmed. Whether it was her natural incli-
nation or some side effect of the vine, she wasn't sure.

"I'm fine. Don't touch me." She said it idly, as if bored by his
concerns.

"What are you doing?"

"Checking the ceiling of course. To make sure it's solid and intact.
I have wonderful plans for this place."

"Are you high?" he blurted.

Dippity was barking his head off like a crazy thing. She laughed at
him.

"Yes, high above the floor."

A vine had wound its way around her arm and up to her armpit.
She giggled at the sensation, shivering.

"When did you learn . . . how to do that?"

"I didn't. It just happened."

"Maybe you should get down."

"Maybe you should mind your own business," she said, swinging
now. Just to see if she could.

The vertiginous feeling of motion high up made her logical brain
quiver, but the part of her connected to the canopy of green wasn't
worried a bit. Thinking of it, she became vaguely aware of the vine
embedded in her knuckle. The original one. She could, if she nar-
rowed down her focus, feel it flexing, expanding and growing.

Changing her.

Pushing Morgan into the vines was the best thing she could have
done for everyone involved. Whether or not the other woman agreed,
or her cheating husband would agree, she knew it in her heart to be
so.

Like a child, she swung her legs up until they caught in the thick
foliage. Immediately vines began to encircle her ankles to hold her.
How free was she now? No expectations from Jace. No worries. No
need to overthink every goddamn thing and feel inferior. No need at
all to worry so much. If she needed support, she had it. If she needed
help, she had it. If she needed a common conscience to boost and
buoy her—she had it.

"Jesus, Bristol!" he yelled.

The dog continued to howl. But as Bristol let go with her hands
and hung from her feet like a child on the playground, she laughed.

This was what life should be like. This was love. This was union.

CHAPTER 44

HIS WIFE WAS HANGING FROM the ceiling and his dog was going insane. Jace had never felt so much like he was in a movie than in that moment. Cheating had been a mistake but the lunacy that followed was ten times more nuts than he could have imagined.

"I think we need to talk," he said. "Maybe you should come down."

Her blue eyes almost glowing like gas flames, she stared down at him. She was upside down.

"Maybe you should come up here," she said. Then she howled with lunatic laughter.

That laugh put the hair on the back of his neck up. It had an echo to it. Like more voices than one talking in unison. Something out of a horror movie.

"Bristol," he shouted, head tossed back. "Are you okay? What's wrong with you?"

She hung there, arms swinging down. So much so that if he reached up they could have touched. The bizarro version of the Sistine Chapel ceiling. Him down below, a mere mortal. The dull-witted Adam. Her hovering above, his demented god.

"Nothing is wrong with me, *husband*."

Her voice was caustic. There was venom in it. Goosebumps sprang up on his body as he looked into those crazed eyes. His neck throbbed where she'd throttled him. He took a step back.

The dog didn't know what to do. He kept rushing forward toward her, hopping, barking, even snarling occasionally, and then backpedaling to put distance between him and his mistress.

"You should shut that dog up," she snarled.

Dippity had always been her dog. Her baby. Her sweet little man. To hear her speak of him that way made his balls want to crawl back into his body. His wife had gone mad. This wasn't anger from infidelity. This wasn't a lust for vengeance or karma. This was something else altogether. Something unnatural.

Dippity ran then. Flat out ran out of the barn, veering to the left back toward home, he assumed. But something made Bristol's head snap around. She literally dropped from the barn ceiling like a spider and landed on her feet. Around her fingers, wrists, and forearms clung vines.

She was wild-eyed and swaying.

"Get that dog," she said. Then ran past him so fast it made his head hurt.

Dippity was sniffing and bouncing at something in the overgrowth of vines. Jace didn't get a good look at it when Bristol hipchecked him out of the way and grabbed for the dog.

This had always been the dachshund's favorite game. When his people ran for him, playfully tried to grab him, and he dodged them gracefully.

Only this time he yelped as he did so. Seemingly terrified of the woman he usually loved more than anything in the world. Certainly, more than Jace.

He ran at his master and when Jace bent to grab him, the dog leapt into his arms.

"Get him *out of here*," she bellowed. "Get him away from my barn. Away from my space."

Jace couldn't take his eyes away from his wife. There were very fine vines, so fine they appeared to be green hairs, twining through her own. A few in her eyebrows. And one, a little bigger than the baby ones, had wormed into her mouth.

He didn't know what was happening, but he left. It seemed like a good idea.

CHAPTER 45

JACE RAN INTO THE HOUSE clutching the dog. He had a sudden certainty Bristol was right behind him. The hair on his neck stood on end so hard it ached. He put the dog down and turned to bolt the door against his monstrous wife.

She's a monster! An actual monster!

He screamed when the woman appeared.

Taking two steps back, he clutched his chest. "Who are you?"

"Margaret," she said. "Your neighbor. Met your wife the other night. And from the looks of you, it's happening again."

"What's happening again?"

"The growth."

"The vines?"

"Yep." She stepped in without being asked and shut the door.

"Did she hurt you?"

"No. She um . . . seemed to want to."

Jace went to the unpacked moving box marked "Booze" and took the lid off. He found a bottle of Basil Hayden and took three hearty swigs directly from the bottle.

He offered his new neighbor a drink.

She waved a wrinkled hand and said, "Don't drink." She then proceeded to take out a pack of cigarettes and light one without asking.

She held the pack out to him, and he shook his head. "Don't smoke."

With a grunt of what seemed disapproval she put them back in the pocket of her faded housecoat.

"I'm your nearest neighbor."

His eyes darted toward the front door and the four small squares of black glass that were open eyes to the dark night outside.

"You can stop staring at the door," she said. "She won't come up here. Not yet. The vines can't travel this far. Not without help."

"Isn't she the help?"

"Yes and no. They're consuming her. Taking her over. Eventually, she'll be able to make her way, but for now, she's kind of tethered to them."

"How do you know this?"

She shrugged her bony shoulders. "I was here the last time. When the McGees went under."

"He went missing and she left!" he barked.

"They charmed him and he went with them. Then I'm pretty sure they got her. All speculation. The only thing I know for certain is that the vines are what we need to worry about. So, let's focus on that."

"Burn it down!" he said.

"Now why hadn't I thought of that!" she said, laughing. Then shook her head at his perplexed look. "Don't work. I mean, not really. Some of us came up and tried that and the fire just sort of . . . petered out. I figured if there was no one here they just stayed beyond the barrier of the path. Not sure what it is. If there's something hostile to them here or they're enchanted. Rumor had witches around these parts back in the day—"

"Witches!" he blurted. "Enchanted vines? Barriers? What the fuck is happening?"

Another shrug as she squinted one eye and blew out a plume of smoke. "Can't rightfully say except it's bad."

"Thanks for clarifying that."

"I came to warn you. To tell you maybe you should just leave her be. And leave here while you're at it."

"I just sank all my money into this house."

"Well, you can have the house and possibly die in it or leave it and live. Which sounds better to you now?"

He took another huge swallow of Basil Hayden and sighed. "It all sounds like bullshit."

"And yet, here we are."

"What do I do?"

"Keep the doors locked for now. Got any vinegar?"

"Vinegar!"

"Yep, kills on contact. But remember that. On contact. It will only kill what it touches. I like a nice mix of vinegar and dish soap. Hillbilly weed killer." She laughed.

"On a nice side salad," Jace said, laughing with her.

"It works. But only on what it touches. So do herbicides and all that but not as well for some reason. Bleach can work in a pinch. I don't think this is a normal everyday vine."

"Ya think?" Hysterical laughter bubbled out of him, and he couldn't suppress it.

She studied him coolly. "Hysterics won't help, sir."

He sat down heavily and sighed. "What the actual fuck?"

"Indeed."

She walked past him, turned on the tap, and put the cigarette out. He heard it hiss.

Then she said, "I'll come back to check on you tomorrow."

"If I'm here," he said sarcastically.

"Yep. If you're here." She said it without sarcasm.

He was fucked.

After she left, he sat and stared at those dark squares of glass before finally getting up and covering the windowpanes with a throw blanket hung crudely on the fixtures still attached to the door.

For some reason, in his mind's eye, he saw Bristol's face, otherworldly and changed forever pressed to the window glass. He feared if he imagined it enough times, it would come to fruition. Like thinking yourself thin, or positive thinking your way to rich.

"Imagine yourself murdered," he said and finally turned his back on the shrouded door.

In the kitchen he checked the back door. Then he stumbled over something. Bristol's tote bag. When he hung it up on the back of the chair, he felt the weight of it and looked inside.

A dark brown leather-bound book.

He opened it to where it was bookmarked with a napkin and started to read.

CHAPTER 46

I THINK THERE'S MORE GOING on out in the barn than grief and planning. Cecil has come in with some wounds and is very secretive now. Too secretive for someone who's just working on a project.

He never told me what project. I assumed it was some sort of workshop. Or maybe even planning for some large garden beds we discussed long ago. The other day I noticed something peeking out from beneath his skin, and thinking he had a splinter, a rather large one, I rushed to him to try and help.

He snatched his hand back, practically snarling at me, and said he was fine. That he could get it out himself. Then disappeared into the bathroom and shut the door.

Hours later when he returned his hand was swaddled as if it had been terribly burned. Way too much bandaging for a mere splinter.

I asked him what he'd done and he said it was fine. He'd removed it and cleaned it and was simply erring on the side of caution. Admitting he was a bit paranoid ever since he got that bout of antibiotic-resistant cellulitis from a carpentry

wound.
 He was lying. I know my husband and he was lying. There is something else going on here and I fear, in my heart of hearts, it is way worse than drinking, gambling, or infidelity.
 And I don't know what to do.
 The only thing I can really think of now is to go out there when he's out there but occupied. Spying feels like a terrible thing but I'm at a loss! I wish he'd just talk to me and tell me what's going on!
 More later.

CHAPTER 47

FRIDAY

BRISTOL WOKE WITH DEW ON her face. She was lying in a tangle of vines not far from the barn. To all sides of her, the tender ends of vines waved in the air, seeking. She watched them for a moment, mesmerized, feeling a lethargic sense of awe.

They had wound all around her body but not tightly. When she turned, she felt the release of the vines.

So, this was what it was like to be accepted—no expectations.

Vines just like the ones embedded in the skin of her hands were now working their way around her legs. The beginnings of an internal network at one with her system.

She flexed her toes, feeling the tug of vegetal material in her body. Some of the leaves near the top of her thigh tickled at her crotch but she felt no worry or fear. They would go where they wanted and settle there. They would become part of her and she them. If they worked together, they could break the barrier she felt had kept them at bay and at home by the barn. They could work their way to the house, the neighbor, the town beyond.

Working together.

She rolled to her belly and stood slowly. Farther into the woods was a creek and she walked toward the sound of its whispering waters. She knelt, scooped up a handful of water, and sipped from her palm. It was good—cold and minerally. She immediately repeated the process. Turning her face to the sun, she soaked in the warmth. It wasn't hot yet, just balmy, and she relished the combination of cool water and warm sun.

After communing with the woods for a moment, she went to check on Morgan. The woman had ceased to move. Thick vines, as big around as a magic marker, had wormed into her eyes, forcing the soft globes to pop. Some of the vitreous humor had run down her cheeks like ghostly tears. The thickest branch by far, as big around as a toilet paper tube, had pushed into her mouth, her tongue poked comically to one side, her lips splitting at the seams reminding Bristol of a Glasgow smile. She tapped the vine-covered head of her husband's mistress.

"And this, dearie, is why you don't fuck with Mother Nature."

At the words, the vines around her legs shifted and rose higher. The end of one swaying near the opening of her vagina. Where her underwear had once resided but were now absent.

Was that it? Was she to be a mother after all? Mother to something virulent, fast, and consuming? Was she to be the mother of the woods?

She cocked her head and listened. From her new home she had already vacated came the sounds of Dippity barking. She wondered if Jace had remained or fled like the coward he was. It wouldn't surprise her to learn he'd left their dog to his own devices. If Dippity was more accepting of her new nature she'd go get him. Bring him into the fold. But he wasn't and that was a bad idea.

Just enough humanity remained in her to leave him be. She'd get back to work growing her community. As she tiptoed farther along the path, the vines crept with her.

CHAPTER 48

THERE HAD TO BE BLEACH in the house. Or vinegar, for fuck's sake.

Jace ripped the lids off boxes looking for cleaning supplies and kitchen staples. He flung them over his shoulder, looking like a madman—which he'd become. He muttered to himself as he worked.

"This was not what I expected. *None of this* is what I expected."

Reading that damned journal had made what was already awful that much worse. Fear was deeply rooted in him now. A hot barb stuck in his gut.

Meanwhile, the dachshund had taken to standing at the front door, faced toward where the path to the woods was beyond the door's confines, barking furiously and constantly.

"For fuck's sake, Dippity! Stop!" he shouted.

The dog froze for a moment, regarded his human, and resumed making noise.

Short of taping Dippity's muzzle shut, there was nothing to be done about it. He tried to tune him out.

In one of the boxes, he found a bottle of oven cleaner. When he read the ingredients, he doubted any would help him. Not to mention, he didn't know what most of them were and he didn't have time to stand and Google each one.

If he went to the grocery store, would it be safe? Would she come into the house while he was gone? He didn't know but he had to do something. Spraying oven cleaner on his vine-infested wife didn't seem like it would do much good at all.

He nearly fell down the basement steps going to the laundry area, praying for bleach.

Nothing.

Then he rummaged under the utility sink hoping for some gardening items. That was a bust. Lots and lots of air fresheners because Bristol hated them all and rarely used the bottle more than once.

There were varying bottles of things that might be slightly flammable but no guarantee they'd work. He'd need to leave. To go to the grocery store. Or the small stop and shop nearby—if it was open. It was run by retirees and the hours were at their whim.

"Fuck. Fuck fuck fuck!"

Jace took a moment to have a mini temper tantrum before catching his breath.

"Okay. Calm down. Maybe if we could capture her and get her to a doctor."

But if the neighbor, Margaret, was to be believed that wouldn't be possible.

Was he really going to *murder* his wife? That's pretty much what it would come down to, wouldn't it? Killing her?

He didn't know if he wanted to kill her but he did want to protect himself from her. Because not only was Bristol still hurt and pissed off at him, she now appeared to be some kind of mutant woman. And if you've ever seen a mutant movie . . . things rarely end well.

CHAPTER 49

SOMEONE WAS COMING. SHE FELT it. The whole of the thatch of green seemed to ripple with it. Bristol shut her eyes and listened with all of herself.

Footsteps, but not from the house. This time they approached from another direction, coming through the woods to the east.

What was over there? She had no idea. She hadn't strayed that way and neither had the vines. They'd been here before the barn, before the house, when once just a small shack lay here. She'd seen all this as she slept, assuming the images had come down the vines like electricity down a live wire.

The woman who had lived there long ago, even before the McGees had come along, lost her daughter and then her cat to the vines. And she had known things. She'd been the kind of woman the town talked about. All atwitter about women and practices that went against God and their holy book. She'd known things that could keep the vines contained. And so here they sat. Just needing a guide to take them farther down the path, to bypass the boundaries set by that woman.

A shiver ran through her and echoed along the vegetal chain of the vines. She ached to get up and approach but was reassured it was better to wait.

A head poked into the clearing to the right of the barn. Bristol watched silently. She recognized the face but at first the name wouldn't come to her. Then she remembered.

Margaret.

The neighbor woman.

Evidently, their new house had come with an incorrigible nosy neighbor.

She waited, feeling the ripple of recognition and concern through the canopy. What was this intrusive woman doing here?

Moving slowly, Bristol disengaged from the cluster of greenery she'd been resting in.

She turned with great care to not draw attention to herself. She felt the vines that had embedded themselves into her calves and up her thighs flex. A slight tugging sensation that wasn't painful but wasn't pleasurable either. She was being absorbed but still felt different. Other.

The tug was also inside her, running up to the empty womb that had been such an intense issue with her traitorous husband.

Was Margaret here to harm them? Was Margaret here to assess? What did she want and how could they get her to go away?

There was only one way to soothe her soul and that was to protect what was hers and what had taken her as its. She wouldn't let this troublesome neighbor ruin what she had found.

Margaret went to the barn. A soft ripple went through the network. Something an observer would pass off as a breeze passing through.

"Are you here?" the woman called softly. She waited and then said, "If you're still even you, that is."

She waited as if Bristol would answer her. Bristol simply watched. The woman held something in each hand, and she couldn't quite make it out.

Again, the woman spoke as if in the middle of a perfectly normal conversation.

"Cecil was overcome. I like to think if me and Marielle had paid more attention he could have made it. But who's to say? And in the end, this cluster of green weirdness claimed her too. So I've stayed far away."

She walked toward one of the ladders and examined it.

Worry shunted through Bristol and the vines responded. Tightening as if holding their breath.

The woman stepped onto the ladder but stopped on the second rung.

"I should have come out here and taken care of things, but I figured the house would never sell. Standing empty for so long. Way out here. No one was really marketing it. But I was mistaken, and some damn fool bought the land at auction from a distant relative who decided to try selling it. And your dumb ass husband bought it."

Bristol nearly laughed at that.

"I guess, it is true, you get what you pay for. He got it for a steal and now it's stolen his life. Aided by his stupidity, the depths of which I have yet to plumb, I assume."

True, Bristol thought.

She moved slowly. The sound of her like tree leaves rustling in the breeze. There were no small animals to flee from her movement. No birds to take flight. Not even the high screaming song of the cicadas could be heard in this part of the woods.

"I wish I knew what this stuff was," the woman said, looking up at the canopy. "But I've always been into science myself. So I'm going to experiment."

The spray bottle she held tottered in her hand as she held on to keep her balance while looking up.

She sprayed a fast, heavy stream and watched the vines she hit twist and wither.

The sensation was sudden and consuming. Burning. And the smell . . . the smell was familiar to Bristol. The part of her who was still a hardworking, cheated-on, entrepreneurial woman and not vine.

Vinegar.

The woman sprayed again in a fresh spot. The vines rippled like a field of wheat and the pain flared again, hitting Bristol in all the places the vines had burrowed their tiny fingers into. A searing pain filled her, but she knew, somehow, that it was referred pain. Like when your ear aches from a bad tooth. She was not being burned. Not yet. She was just feeling the pain of the afflicted vegetation.

The woman let the bottle drop and Bristol felt the mass of vines relax as if exhaling, herself included.

"No good scientist just tries one thing." Bristol watched her raise the other spray bottle and give a few spritzes.

This time a roar, unheard by human ears, but felt by the entity, went up.

That's straight alcohol. I think there must be something better, and getting your hands on that much alcohol would be a feat, but we'll see.

A rustling started. Vines, both young and petites and older and thick, waved in the air, seeking purchase. One hovered dangerously close to the woman's unruly silver hair.

Bristol held her breath. Waiting. Waiting for the vines to strike.

Before they could, the woman, like a gunslinger from an old movie shooting double-fisted, sprayed a combination of vinegar and alcohol at anything approaching her.

"Smells like a pickle went to the doctor for a shot," she said, laughing.

Then she stepped off the ladder carefully and ran down the path toward the house. Beyond their boundaries. Farther than they could go.

For now.

CHAPTER 50

BRISTOL WATCHED HER GO, RUNNING like a child instead of an old woman. Something in her admired Margaret. Wished maybe she'd seen that quality before she'd started to change.

The vines along her legs itched, moving slowly, creeping. Inside her, she felt a similar stirring. A puncturing pain that made her worry she wouldn't make the transition.

Between her legs, blood flowed, and she thought about how familiar that was. Blood flowing down her thighs, surprising her, cramping her, clots and gushes of blood. Every month. Disappointing her. Disappointing the man who claimed to love her.

But now her womb was useful. Now her womb was inhabited. Not all the way, but close. She would be the thing to break the barrier. To walk the throng of green and brown up the trail to the house, through the fields, to the town.

They would grow unimpeded and free, as intended. They would

be the thing to fear. They would be the thing that overtook all other things.

She wasn't sure why this made her happy. A part of her mind that was still Bristol, still human, still caring and empathetic and fearful, thought she should kill herself here and now.

But then more vines crept up along her back, across her shoulders, caressing her, comforting her. Accepting her.

CHAPTER 51

MARGARET BURST INTO THE HOUSE and the dog went insane. "Hey, Mr. What's Your Name? Jack!"

No answer.

"Hush!" she said deeply to the barking dog and low and behold he did. "Good boy."

She looked outside only to see no vehicle. The man was gone.

"Did that coward flee?"

The dog cocked his head, and she sighed. "I guess not. I do think he's a coward, but I don't think he'd leave you if he was running. He must be coming back."

She went out the back door, the short black and tan dachshund on her heels. He was panting in the heat and from all the barking.

"Give me a minute and I'll get you some water, bub. You need to calm down some."

He stayed close to her, and she felt just a tiny hint of affection.

She'd denied herself a dog for years but could tell this little guy was scared.

The shed she remembered from Cecil and Marielle's day was still there, looking worse for wear. She tried to open it and it was locked. "Oh, come the fuck on."

The hasp on the lock was rusted as all get out so Margaret planted her foot against the shed door and grabbed the handle and pulled as hard as she could while bracing her foot on the dry rotted wood.

The handle came off and she let out a grunt as she fell on her ass in the dry brown grass.

She shook off the dog who was desperately trying to lick her. Margaret climbed to her feet and stomped to the side of the shed. She grabbed a shovel that had been abandoned in the grass.

She wedged the head of the shovel between the doors and again began to lean back with all her weight. Which was more considerable than it once had been. A fact she was, in that moment, grateful for.

The door flew open, and she paused to catch her breath. She couldn't use anything electric. She needed an old-school manual.

Perfect. Clippers. Big old ones that could probably decapitate someone. She spotted WD-40 and drenched the blade and its hinge with the oily substance, opening and closing them enough to get them working smoothly.

"What the hell are you doing?"

She whirled around, brandishing the clippers wildly.

The homeowner jumped back and put his hands up.

"Don't sneak up on someone like that!" she said. "Jesus, I could have killed you."

"What are those for?"

"The vines. Where were you? Your dog was going insane."

Dippity was seated by her right leg watching the back and forth.

"The grocery store. I was getting a few things."

He turned to head toward the house, and Margaret followed.

CHAPTER 52

IN THE KITCHEN WERE GALLONS and gallons of white vinegar and a couple family-size bottles of dish soap.

"My mother used to do it so I guess it should work?" he said softly.

"Good old-fashioned weed killer," she said.

"Yes."

"And how do you propose we dispense this? How's your trigger finger? Ready to do a recreation of the O.K. Corral? Can you squeeze a spray bottle a couple thousand times in a row? 'Cause my arthritis is pretty gnarly."

Jace shook his head. "The garden center is near the grocery. So, I popped in."

She chuckled. He'd bought actual spraying tanks. She was reminded of a movie from the nineties where John Goodman played a bumbling exterminator.

"That should work," she admitted.

"When do we go?"

"Dusk maybe? Sun's not out, they should be dormant. They're creatures of heat and light." Margaret shrugged. "Of course, that's just a guess on my part."

"It's the best we have."

She cocked her head. "Did you do something to your wife? Something to make her easy for them to take down."

He shook his head and then thought better of it. "I cheated," he confessed to Margaret.

She grunted. "Those things, whatever they are, will eat her up and then they'll come for you. For me. And beyond."

"Where did they come from?"

"Fuck if I know. But they're here and that's what we need to worry about."

It took them almost an hour to fill all the canisters. A jug of vinegar, half a jug of water, and a hefty stream of dish soap. When all was said and done, they had four canisters. When given the number of vines out there on the barn, in the barn, and seemingly traveling toward the house, Margaret felt pretty certain they were fucked. And she said so.

Jace nodded. "How are we getting this all down there? We certainly can't carry it."

"And not with clippers too. There's only one pair so we'll have to take turns."

He shook his head. "Hold on."

Jace went and rummaged through one of the still-full moving boxes. He came back with a long sharp knife and a grin.

"What the fuck is that?"

"My machete," he said.

"No offense, but why, city boy, do you have a machete?"

He smiled. "Because you never know when you're going to need one."

She couldn't argue with that.

CHAPTER 53

WHEN DUSK WAS FINALLY CREEPING around them, Margaret told Jace she was going to head back to the house to get her pickup. Jace watched her go, feeling a bit surreal. Was this really happening? Was he having some bizarre guilt-induced dream?

He waited by the door for Margaret to return while the dog sat at his feet whining.

"What do I do with you?" he asked. "Leave you here? What if something happens to me and that woman? Take you? I don't want you to get hurt. What do I do?"

He'd never felt this unsure, this chaotic inside. And what were they about to do? Go kill some vines or go kill his wife?

Would this be happening if he'd been able to keep his dick in his pants? Jace had no idea but part of him said it wouldn't. This was a direct result of his stupidity.

A deep rumble broke the silence. He heard the truck before he saw it. Then it pulled up. A beat-up faded red pickup. Dented and spewing grayish-blue smoke behind it.

Margaret got out and lowered the tailgate. Jace grabbed two jugs and went out to load them. She passed him on the way back in to get the machete.

Finally, the truck was loaded and she looked down at Dippity. "What are we doing with him?"

"I don't know. What do you think?"

"Will he go after it if we take him?"

"I have no idea."

She shrugged and looked at the dog. "Go inside."

Dippity looked at her and ran to the truck.

"Well, that solves it," she said, and got in the cab.

Jace pulled the front door closed behind them, wondering if he'd ever see his brand-new house again. Or his wife. Or anything even close to the life he'd planned for them.

CHAPTER 54

DUSK WAS COMING. ALL AROUND her was nothing but fading light, vibrant green, tepid air, and easy motion. Almost like swaying. She could hear gentle reassuring creaks, the vines around her growing. Her vision, with her eyes closed and pierced by bright yellow sunlight, made her feel as if she were underwater. Perhaps at the bottom of a pond during an algae bloom.

But above all else, there was peace.

The retained heat of the vines penetrated her, merging with her, on the verge of being too much but never quite hitting that mark. She tried to relax into it. There wasn't the need to worry or question herself. She simply lay there and became one with nature. With light and heat and green and growth.

A beautiful thing.

She was in a state much like dozing, feeling the soft slide of vegetation along the small of her back, when she heard it.

It was still at a distance but clear and intrusive. The belch and grumble of an old vehicle. Letting loose a plume of toxic smoke, no doubt. Bad for the air, the earth, the wildlife. Just bad.

Not that the vines were good for the wildlife. That's why it was so damn quiet here, always. What hadn't been absorbed had fled in fear. A predator that could be sensed but not necessarily sussed out was a predator to truly be feared.

It had to be Jace. As much of a coward as he was, who else would be riding out here like the calvary? Unless it was Margaret. She was a more feared adversary as far as Bristol was concerned.

She settled there, pushed back in the growth by the side of the barn, wanting to sink into oblivion and let herself go, but fearing it was too soon. That she would be called upon to protect the growth. She couldn't merge too soon anyway, she was still the mobile one. She was their ticket out of this small piece of woods and into the world.

CHAPTER 55

THE DOG WAS GOING INSANE and Jace was pretty sure he was too. Margaret, the militant neighbor he'd just met, was driving the old pickup down the path like she was in a WWII movie and piloting a tank. The bouncing coupled with the anxiety was making him sick. The whole situation was making him sick.

Margaret palmed the dog's head and said softly over the roar of her truck, "You need to hush now."

He marveled when the dog actually hushed.

The tail kept going a million miles an hour and small whines escaped Dippity's throat, but the barking stopped.

"Good boy." Margaret gave him a pat on the butt.

"You're awfully calm," Jace said.

She shrugged. "Not the first time I dealt with these things. I tried to help Marielle back in the day. She told me I was crazy. And then she disappeared. Can't imagine where she went." She rolled her eyes.

"You think the vines got her." It wasn't a question.

"I *know* the vines got her," she replied.

He sighed. They were getting closer and his stomach wanted to crawl right out of his throat, he was so scared. That level of fear had a numbing effect, though. He was starting to fear the vines had gotten Morgan, probably with some help from Bristol.

But if his wife was becoming something like them, was she a murderer? Surely not.

"How can you be sure?"

Another shrug. "I can't. But the last I talked to her, she was going to 'go out to that barn and give Cecil a piece of her mind, tell him he had to stop obsessing'. And I never saw her again. Nobody did."

She coasted to a stop about a hundred yards from the barn.

"This is the barrier now," she said.

She nodded toward the woods bracketing the clearing. "See, they stop right about there."

"Where do they start?"

"Hell if I know! Some of the old timers speculated a meteor crash. Other's black magic. Some said it was nature taking the upper hand back. Nobody *really* knows. All we knew is they had a perimeter. Thanks to that old witchy woman decades ago. Or so they say. Sometimes, I think it's just nature has a mind of its own, and nature must be respected."

"So, when Marielle disappeared, you just, what . . . stayed away?"

"Yep. I stayed away. As long as no one was in that house or in that barn and messing with them, they stayed where they were. Not a lot of wildlife out here, if you notice," she snorted. "But then you came along and bought the damn house and started the whole thing over again."

"It was a really good deal," he mumbled.

"When are people going to learn that often a really good deal comes with a really big headache?"

She cut the engine and Jace cringed because the silence was deafening.

"We have to get out of the car, you know. We have a good amount of light left, but eventually it'll fade."

"Uh-huh," he said.

She opened her door, and he opened his. The creaking of the old Ford steel was ridiculously amplified.

He didn't want to move. His legs felt like lead weights, his heart did that crazy fish flop thing it often did. Every cell in his body was filled with dread.

Then the decision was made for him because a long, lean, brown body leapt free from the cab and barreled toward the barn.

"Dippity!"

CHAPTER 56

THE CREAKING HAD INCREASED AND now there was a rustle. A motion much like the rippling of a wave and Bristol felt it wash over her *and* work through her simultaneously.

She'd faded out again. Now she opened her eyes to a cloud of green and muted light rushing through the surrounding area. She could smell the damp, verdant smell of the vines and the woods. Her eyes struggled to focus on her surroundings. As ruined by vines and crusted over as they were, she found she could still see. Focusing was also necessary for her other senses.

Her ears picked up a familiar and once beloved sound. The yips and barks of Dippity. The scent of car exhaust and burning oil filled her nose. The tang of gasoline.

Oh, dear, didn't come to burn us, did they?

The thought drifted through her consciousness like a leaf on the water.

Worry was very low down on her mental list now. Bliss and joy and peace and silence were what ruled. A community of slow movement and camaraderie.

She heard voices. One of them was Jace, sparking a flare of anger. Another rustle and creak from the brocade of vegetation around her. The places where the vines touched her, twined around her, sunk into her flesh, crept inside her very body, ached. The human part of her was suddenly noticeably different from the new and improved part of her.

She felt a tightening of the tangle attached to her and the rustle of the ones inside her. A pressure and a tightening in her womb, her belly, and in her throat. Her eyes, dotted with flecks of gold and green, strained to see the intruders.

The truck became visible. A once bright red now faded to a dirty pinkish hue. More rust than truck, really.

The woman. The neighbor. Margaret. She remembered her warning and her concern. Her big personality and her brash nature.

Bristol moved slowly, remembering she was now tethered, and must make sure those surrounding her could move with her.

Something in the underbrush scuttled. A cold calcified sound. She snatched it up. A beetle. Into her mouth it went, and she relished the brittle crunch between her teeth and the brackish taste of its vital juices.

The woman wore old jeans and a ripped tee. Her crazy blond-gray hair was twisted up in a knot. She held some kind of canister in her hands as she scanned the woods.

Looking for me, are you?

Bristol knew they were.

Where's Bristol?

She thought of the children's books with the little hidden man and smiled. It would probably be more difficult to find her than to find Waldo.

Then something bounced into the brush and hit her full force. Dippity.

She reached for him, but the tangle of vines slowed her some. He snarled and yipped some more, his bark a cacophony to her mind, now accustomed to the sacred silence of the woods where they resided.

He found her face somehow. What was left of it that hadn't been changed and morphed. He licked her incessantly. Really getting close and nuzzling the way he always had. And suddenly Bristol found the still human part of herself warring with the inhuman.

CHAPTER 57

"DIPPITY! HERE, BOY!" JACE SCREAMED.

Margaret stomped ahead of him, adjusting and testing the nozzle of her sprayer. She wasn't particularly tall, so it was an awkward shuffling walk as she worked it out.

"Hush up!" she snapped.

"That's my dog," he said, working his mister to make sure it worked. The air smelled of caustic vinegar and soap. "He might be the only thing I have left in the world."

He had lost hope for his wife, now one with this wild country growth.

Margaret turned to him, hissing out under her breath. "Shush. Don't get all worked up. And don't worry about that dog. He's smarter than you!"

His mouth clamped shut. Part in fear, part in outrage.

Together they advanced, both surveying exactly where the vines lay. He'd never seen it move. Not particularly far. Not beyond the stray tendrils blowing in a breeze, finding a place to land and attach, which he knew from science class was the way vines grew and advanced. He'd taken that class for the credits to meet his needs. *And look how it's come in handy . . .*

A wild cackling laugh burst out of him. Margaret glared at him as he clapped a hand over his mouth.

"Get a hold of yourself," she said. "Pay attention. I have no idea how this stuff works. I have no idea if it can rush out and get us or what."

He shook his head. "Me either."

"Something tells me your missus communed with it. She went willingly. But that's just speculation and, in this instance, speculation can get you killed."

He had to swallow hard around the lump in his throat.

A river of sweat rolled down his back. He could feel it moving along his skin. The heat had been excessive today and the cicadas screamed in the trees. Their sex, sex, sex and death anthem.

His skin prickled suddenly with goosebumps not just from the temperature but fear. Everything felt cross-wired and for a split second he felt as if the world had tilted under his feet.

Then a stream of warm, rank water hit him. Soap slid into his mouth and his body reeked of vinegar. She'd sprayed him.

"Snap out of it, Skippy. We have work to do. Or these vines are going to get to your house, then mine, then town. You woke them up again, you get to help me stop them."

Then Dippity started barking again and they both moved quickly but carefully toward the sound.

CHAPTER 58

SHE FELT HERSELF SOFTEN. AN unusual feeling for her now. Just days ago, this was her favorite creature and now she had to convince herself to accept his affection. He licked and nuzzled, moving closer.

Around her, the vines stirred. Some snaking closer to her body because of the intruder. She tried to indicate it was fine. He was safe. This was her dog.

"Dippity," she managed. Her voice a garbled mockery of what it once was. A throat that sounded torn and ruined by the thick woody vines that wormed into her mouth and down the sides. But under it all was the original voice. A voice that had once sang him silly songs about being her furry baby boy.

His tail moved incessantly, and she remembered this was a sign of happiness.

And then, as she bent forward to put her face against his, some vines snapped forward, wrapping around his back legs. What had once been her fingertips, now gnarled, extended, and vibrant green, instinctively slipped around his forelegs, gripping him tight, anchoring him.

And Dippity opened his mouth and howled.

Then came pain, coursing red and green in a sea of foliage and dimming daylight. Teeth gnashed at her, her face, her jawline, her breast, her neck. The neck hurt her worst, and she felt the whole of herself and the vines try to recoil. To eject the creature.

He had latched on and as she rose from her lying position and tried to stand as upright as she was able, the dog hung there, teeth embedded. His back end swung, his small body nearly limp as he continued to keep his teeth buried, moving his jaw only enough to mimic chewing. To create more agony and fear for the woman who had once put him in a Santa suit and fed him peanut butter.

CHAPTER 59

JACE SPUN IN A CIRCLE trying to pinpoint the sound, but Margaret already had. She was sending the strongest stream of vinegar and soap she could into the greenery.

Jace felt a giggle bubble up out of him. This was their defense. Regular kitchen staples. Pickling liquid with a dash of fucking soap in it.

He moved forward and sprayed for all he was worth.

"Spread out!" Margaret snarled.

She was right, he thought, blinking. He needed to cover the ground she wasn't, not bunch up behind her.

"Sorry, sorry . . ." he muttered and moved to the left.

Spraying wildly, watching the liquid hit vines and sparkle in the remaining light, he thought how mad this was. Thinking this wouldn't accomplish anything at all.

Margaret was whistling like a truck driver, a high-pitched whistle to call the dog from the overgrown area.

"Come on, Dippity! Come here, boy!" Jace added his voice to the fray.

Somewhere under the chaos overlaid with forestry hush, he heard another sound. A scream maybe. A high pitch that made his ears ache and his teeth sing.

Then a groan.

Then a dark bullet of a dog came rushing from the vines. Leaves clung to his paws, a piece of woody vine stuck out of his mouth. He looked rumpled as he jumped at Jace but unhurt for the most part.

Jace stuck a hand out wildly to try and catch the canine projectile and managed to snatch the sausage body from the air. Dippity was hot and shaking. He was a mass of energy in a small package.

Jace continued to spray, setting the dog at his feet and snarling, "Stay."

Sometimes if you used the mean voice the dog would listen.

Margaret had dropped her first canister and was headed back to the truck for her second when a vine whipped forward, so fast it made a whistling sound, and caught around her leg.

"Shit," Jace said.

Things were getting out of hand.

He found the machete along the back of his belt and pulled it free. Aiming as well as he could while shaking so hard, he brought it down near Margaret's bound leg and severed the vine.

The remainder retracted like an octopus tentacle in a horror movie.

Margaret found her footing, grunting with the effort, and hustled to the truck. She grabbed her canister and said, "I'd say thanks, but I'll save that for if we actually get out of this shit show alive."

Nudging Dippity gently aside with his boot, he advanced and began to spray. Maybe if he sprayed long enough he'd find his wife and get her back. What was left of her.

CHAPTER 60

MARGARET GLANCED AT WHAT WAS left in her canister as she attempted to spray the vines creeping up the back and side of the barn.

What had they been thinking? This was nowhere near enough to kill all this. The vision of the vines was deceiving. They were dense and intertwined and as she studied, keeping a very mindful eye on the ground where they could advance on her, she saw they climbed the nearest trees and crept into their summer canopies. They had strangled out other plants and bushes and wound gaily around the trunks of young trees. They were everywhere.

And in it somewhere was Bristol. She was part of them now. Fully part, Margaret feared. She'd been out here too long.

The dog sat on the far perimeter whimpering. From his mouth hung bits of gray and brown bark and green leaves. He didn't shake it off and didn't eat it either. She let it lie there as if in penance.

"You gave her a run for her money, didn't you, boy?" she muttered.

The smell of vinegar was overwhelming, and Margaret wondered if she'd ever eat a pickle again without gagging.

Probably not.

She advanced a few more feet toward the corner of the barn and thought about the other jugs in her truck. Big red jugs of gasoline. A last-ditch effort. It hadn't rained for a piece and setting fire to the woods was risky. It could spread. Equally risky was setting fire to the woods and quickly attracting the attention of the local fire department. Then the fire couldn't do its job.

The more she studied the wooded area, the more she feared vinegar and soap wasn't going to cut it. Not unless they had a truckload.

"Be careful they don't snake out and get ya!" she yelled to Jace.

Not a second later one of them unfurled quickly and wound around his wrist so fast it seemed impossible. He yelled, the dog jumped, sinking his teeth in, hanging from the vine like he had a death wish. Savaging the greenery with his small teeth.

Jace, for once quick thinking, took the machete and cut the vine just below the hanging dog. The remainder withdrew quickly, leaving green juice on the dry dirt as it left.

"You good?" she asked him. He gave a nod and turned to another section of trees.

She backed up, trying to assess where she should spray next. A hand fell on Margaret's shoulder. A hand now swathed in rich green leaves and thin gnarled bark.

"Margaret—"

It was the missus. When she turned to break her grip and face her, the woman was a monstrosity. Her eyes shot through with thin woody tendrils. Clear jelly leaked down her cheeks in horrifying threads. Blood made a snail's trail down her face and neck.

Her body trying to heal itself, Margaret thought frantically.

Bristol's mouth was stuffed full of greenery to the point it would have been comical had it not been so dreadful. Her throat was a tapestry of invading vines. Her tongue was barely able to move.

She groped for Margaret and the woman managed to fall back.

"No offense, Bristol, I know we only met once, but you look like hell."

She sprayed her full in the face with the concoction on the highest spray setting. It seemed useless. Like throwing teaspoons of water on a raging inferno but she did it until the thing that had once been her neighbor stumbled back into the camouflage of green.

As she was swallowed up once more, Margaret noted her legs were a barbed wire network of vines and tendrils. The thickest of them tented her dress obscenely and Margaret wondered how full of vine this poor woman was. How far she had gone.

She knew in her heart there was no turning back.

And suddenly, in reaction to the attack, larger areas of vines began to creep forward, advancing on them from the cool darkness of the woods.

Margaret yelled to Jace. "Go to the truck. Fuck this. It's time for Plan B!"

She didn't have to tell him twice.

CHAPTER 61

SHE TIPPED OUT THE REMAINDER of her vinegar concoction and began pouring gasoline in to replace it.

"Don't just stand there and stare at me. Do the same. And get those other two canisters."

They worked silently, listening for anything odd, one eye on the forest.

"Was that . . . was that her?"

"It was."

"Was she—?"

"She's gone. She's just a transport system now. Let her go. We can't hurt her now. We can only help her with this." She gave a brisk nod at the sprayers now filled with amber fluid.

She turned to Jace, who seemed to be in shock, and pointed a finger at him. "Do not. *Do. Not.* Get this on you. Because once we spray it, I'm lighting this fucker up."

He stared at her. "But Bristol—"

"Is gone," she interjected. "You didn't see her, but I did. She is not Bristol anymore, hon. She is gone. You need to remember that."

Dippity was barking his ass off. The vines, now realizing the threat, moved forward from the tree line. A bizarre scene in the now purpling twilight.

"Let's go," Margaret said. "Start spraying. Keep clear. Don't get it on you. And when you're out of gas, let me know."

"I thought this didn't work in the past?"

"It didn't. But we need to try something, so I'll believe it will fail when it actually fails. Got it??"

He nodded dumbly. "Got it."

She moved forward into the barn. Very wary. Very alert. Raising the nozzle, she let loose a strong stream of gas. The reek was overwhelming, and she paused to raise her shirt collar over her nose and mouth.

When she was satisfied, she backed out and moved to the right of the barn, spraying the tree line until she ran out of gas. After gathering her second canister she returned and sprayed until she hit the line of delineation. It was farther than it once had been, and she sighed.

This had to work. Had to. All these years dormant. All these years with no one coming out here. And now she'd have to burn the whole thing down. Burn it to save her house, the town, and countless lives.

"Motherfucker," Margaret said and sighed.

CHAPTER 62

JACE LET OUT A SCREAM and stumbled back, almost sloshing the gas on himself. Behind him, at a safe distance, Dippity barked endlessly.

"Jace? Baby? Come to me," she said.

Her body was a mass of gore and vines. Sprouts burst from beneath her cracked fingertips. Her pseudo walk was stiff from the thick stems racing along her calves and up her thighs. Her voice like a gurgling drain.

"Oh, honey," he said on a sob.

She tried to smile, and the sight turned his stomach and made his head ache. A scream built in him as he studied cracked, busted, and missing teeth. A maw full of blood and mucus and vibrant green buds. She was more plant than woman. More invaded than not.

He took a step back, steeling himself.

"We can work it out," she said, her voice a mockery of the voice that once belonged to his best friend.

A day ago, he'd have given anything—anything at all—to hear her say that. To be given the grace of another chance.

Now he knew it was just a lie. A lure.

"I know," he lied.

She smiled wider and a split raced up from her mutilated mouth and burst her cheek apart from lips almost to her ear.

Raw meat gaped at him. He gagged, and before he could change his mind, aimed a line of gasoline toward her.

It hit her full in the face and she recoiled. The vegetation now part of her trembled with the force of the liquid as if under the deluge of rain.

"No," she said.

"I'm sorry," he sobbed. "For everything. Not just this."

"This is all because of you," she said.

The stream found her again and she stumbled back, fell, and was once again absorbed by the boundary of woods and trees and thick lush vines.

He sprayed until he'd emptied both canisters and then, eyes blurry from tears and fumes, ran toward Margaret when she called.

CHAPTER 63

"LET'S GO!" MARGARET BELLOWED.

The dachshund heeded her call first, galloping at full tilt for her, and when she pointed, he leapt into her truck and up onto the seat.

"Good trick, little man," she said.

Jace came racing toward her, dropped his canisters in the truck bed, and barely managed to catch the box of matches she threw at him.

She had a box herself.

Striking her match, she nodded to him to do the same.

He struck the match with shaking hands.

"Ready?"

Together they tossed the matches toward the gas-soaked vines.

They fell short. And went out.

"Well, fuck," Margaret said.

Together they moved closer. Margaret took the lead, taking a bundle of three matchsticks and lighting them. When he mimicked her, they moved forward a little more slowly and dropped them.

They caught. A soft but audible "whoomph" of the fire catching and then she grabbed his arm. "Time to go."

"What if it doesn't—?"

Margaret nodded at the fire racing along the line of gasoline.

"If we have to come back, we will, but I think for now we should beat feet."

Something in the barn caught and a huge arc of fire rose. That was all it took for Jace to get moving.

From the cab of the truck, they watched the burn continue. She caught him swiping at his face.

"If it's any consolation, I think your wife, the woman inside, was gone before we set fire to all this. She wasn't herself anymore. Remember that."

He nodded.

Dippity settled between them, curling into a shrimp shape with a long exhalation of exhaustion.

Margaret kept her eye on the rearview as they drove slowly home. Watching for any fire trucks or responders.

No one came.

CHAPTER 64

FIRE IS BRIGHTER THAN SUNLIGHT, she thinks.

CHAPTER 65

HE'D WATCHED THE WOODS BURN from the front porch. The dog was a wriggling mess of anxiety and whining. Jace did his best to calm him, but after the day they'd had he didn't blame the dog for being upset.

The stink of burning greenery and gasoline filled the air, and to his shock, no fire trucks came, no police.

Maybe they were out far enough it hadn't been noticed yet. Maybe luck was just on their side.

When dusk fell the sight of the fire and the black belches of smoke calmed him. How long would it burn? How far would it go?

He picked up the dog and his whiskey glass, now dry as a bone, and headed inside.

His head ached and so did his heart. He wasn't stupid enough not to realize this was all his fault. He was also smart enough to know he couldn't go back and change anything.

The dream of a baby, a family, and happiness in this old farmhouse was now a distant memory that stank of woodsmoke and accelerants.

After pouring himself another whiskey, he trudged upstairs, stripped off his clothes, shoved them in the bathroom wastebasket and climbed into the shower. He stood under the hot spray for what felt like an eternity, and despite the heat of the day and the heat of the fire, stayed there until the hot water ran out and the water ran cold.

When he finally emerged into the steamy bathroom, he was clean but no more clear-headed or hearted.

He downed the last of his existing whiskey and swore to himself he wouldn't drink anymore.

When he crawled into bed, the dog jumped up with him and curled up in Bristol's spot.

That was nice. He was used to a presence there and at least the little dog gave him that security.

Despite his mind going a million miles a minute, he somehow fell asleep almost instantly. It was a relief to lose consciousness.

CHAPTER 66

IT WAS THE TICKLING THAT woke him.

"Dippity?" he asked hopefully. But his gut and the goosebumps on his shoulders and arms told him it was wishful thinking.

Her breath was hot on the back of his neck. He didn't want to turn, but in the end, he had to.

Her eyes were gone. A milky glow around the protruding bud and leaves. Her mouth was stuffed with growth and her tongue lolled out one side. She managed around it.

"Husband."

His whole body shivered, and he tried very suddenly to pull back from her but she'd wound her tendrils around his arms, shoulders, and calves. He was, in fact, bound tight.

"Bristol—" he started but a vine writhed out from around her neck and caressed his face. He clamped his mouth shut and pressed his lips tight together.

She pulled back a bit and let him see more of her. He wished she hadn't. As bizarre of a visual it was, she rose and stood over him while the long tendrils and whippets of woody vine held him fast. She was a miracle of vegetation and very little human.

The bodice of her dress was ripped, breasts free and bound with vines like deep-cutting tattoos. Her belly swelled with the growth inside her, her upper thighs a fecund mass of leaves.

"I've come to realize how you were right. About us creating life. About us being a family," she said, a garbled monstrous voice clogged with flora. But somehow, he felt he was hearing her more in his head than with his ears.

His balls tried to crawl up inside his body and he tried to back pedal but the bonds around him tightened up.

Jace heard a sob and realized it was him.

She leaned over him. A parody in green and brown of the woman he had loved and ultimately betrayed.

Her dress strained in that way he'd always wished to see it. A ripe round belly below full breasts.

A laugh leaked out of her as he said, "Please—"

She placed a finger on his lips and said, "I'm going to give you what you always wanted. I know how important it is now. Bearing life. Carrying it, propagating it, bringing something forth into the world."

She smiled and he screamed. Blood had dried on her body everywhere the vines had penetrated. Scabs lived on her skin and milky pus decorated her like macabre paint.

"I think it's important we have that bond," she said. The dress began to rustle and tent along the midriff.

He pedaled his feet on the bed but managed to get nowhere.

Though her mouth strained with speech, he understood every single awful word.

"I think you, dear husband, should help me carry this life. Bear it. Then we can be the family you always wanted."

The vines finally strained her dress too far and shot toward him at a terrifying speed. They pushed against his t-shirt and through it. Against his skin and then through that as well.

He could hear their terrible growth, so fast and intense they creaked.

The scream ripping out of him turned his throat to fire.

He felt the vines inside him. Writhing and moving like curious worms. He sobbed as she leaned over him, the tendrils from her belly working their way deep into his. When she smiled warm fluid dripped down on him from her face. Whether it was saliva, tears, or blood, he didn't know.

"Darling," she said. "We have gotten beyond the boundary from the forest. And now, just like you wanted, we will be a family."

ACKNOWLEDGMENTS

Thanks to my epically smart, strong, talented daughter for being part of my inspiration not just in my writing, but in my life. Thanks to my son for being my test pancake—I am so thrilled with the happiness he's found for himself. Thanks to my husband who is my biggest cheerleader and a most dedicated proofreader. And in honor of all the women out there who fight every day to persevere, be heard, and simply exist.

As always, thanks go to Grindhouse Press for giving another of my strange little books a home. It's an honor.

Other Grindhouse Press Titles

www.ingramcontent.com/pod-product-compliance
Lightning Source LLC
Chambersburg PA
CBHW011518240626
47154CB00010B/3077